THE

GIRL

HE

PINED

(A Paige King Mystery—Book One)

BLAKE PIERCE

Blake Pierce

Blake Pierce is the USA Today bestselling author of the RILEY PAGE mystery series, which includes seventeen books. Blake Pierce is also the author of the MACKENZIE WHITE mystery series, comprising fourteen books; of the AVERY BLACK mystery series, comprising six books; of the KERI LOCKE mystery series, comprising five books; of the MAKING OF RILEY PAIGE mystery series, comprising six books; of the KATE WISE mystery series, comprising seven books; of the CHLOE FINE psychological suspense mystery, comprising six books; of the JESSE HUNT psychological suspense thriller series, comprising twenty four books; of the AU PAIR psychological suspense thriller series, comprising three books; of the ZOE PRIME mystery series, comprising six books; of the ADELE SHARP mystery series, comprising fifteen books, of the EUROPEAN VOYAGE cozy mystery series, comprising four books; of the new LAURA FROST FBI suspense thriller, comprising nine books (and counting); of the new ELLA DARK FBI suspense thriller, comprising eleven books (and counting); of the A YEAR IN EUROPE cozy mystery series, comprising nine books, of the AVA GOLD mystery series, comprising six books (and counting); of the RACHEL GIFT mystery series, comprising six books (and counting); of the VALERIE LAW mystery series, comprising three books (and counting); and of the PAIGE KING mystery series, comprising three books (and counting).

An avid reader and lifelong fan of the mystery and thriller genres, Blake loves to hear from you, so please feel free to visit www.blakepierceauthor.com to learn more and stay in touch.

BOOKS BY BLAKE PIERCE

PAIGE KING MYSTERY SERIES
THE GIRL HE PINED (Book #1)
THE GIRL HE CHOSE (Book #2)
THE GIRL HE TOOK (Book #3)

VALERIE LAW MYSTERY SERIES
NO MERCY (Book #1)
NO PITY (Book #2)
NO FEAR (Book #3

RACHEL GIFT MYSTERY SERIES
HER LAST WISH (Book #1)
HER LAST CHANCE (Book #2)
HER LAST HOPE (Book #3)
HER LAST FEAR (Book #4)
HER LAST CHOICE (Book #5)
HER LAST BREATH (Book #6)

AVA GOLD MYSTERY SERIES
CITY OF PREY (Book #1)
CITY OF FEAR (Book #2)
CITY OF BONES (Book #3)
CITY OF GHOSTS (Book #4)
CITY OF DEATH (Book #5)
CITY OF VICE (Book #6)

A YEAR IN EUROPE
A MURDER IN PARIS (Book #1)
DEATH IN FLORENCE (Book #2)
VENGEANCE IN VIENNA (Book #3)
A FATALITY IN SPAIN (Book #4)

ELLA DARK FBI SUSPENSE THRILLER
GIRL, ALONE (Book #1)

GIRL, TAKEN (Book #2)
GIRL, HUNTED (Book #3)
GIRL, SILENCED (Book #4)
GIRL, VANISHED (Book 5)
GIRL ERASED (Book #6)
GIRL, FORSAKEN (Book #7)
GIRL, TRAPPED (Book #8)
GIRL, EXPENDABLE (Book #9)
GIRL, ESCAPED (Book #10)
GIRL, HIS (Book #11)

LAURA FROST FBI SUSPENSE THRILLER
ALREADY GONE (Book #1)
ALREADY SEEN (Book #2)
ALREADY TRAPPED (Book #3)
ALREADY MISSING (Book #4)
ALREADY DEAD (Book #5)
ALREADY TAKEN (Book #6)
ALREADY CHOSEN (Book #7)
ALREADY LOST (Book #8)
ALREADY HIS (Book #9)

EUROPEAN VOYAGE COZY MYSTERY SERIES
MURDER (AND BAKLAVA) (Book #1)
DEATH (AND APPLE STRUDEL) (Book #2)
CRIME (AND LAGER) (Book #3)
MISFORTUNE (AND GOUDA) (Book #4)
CALAMITY (AND A DANISH) (Book #5)
MAYHEM (AND HERRING) (Book #6)

ADELE SHARP MYSTERY SERIES
LEFT TO DIE (Book #1)
LEFT TO RUN (Book #2)
LEFT TO HIDE (Book #3)
LEFT TO KILL (Book #4)
LEFT TO MURDER (Book #5)
LEFT TO ENVY (Book #6)
LEFT TO LAPSE (Book #7)
LEFT TO VANISH (Book #8)

LEFT TO HUNT (Book #9)
LEFT TO FEAR (Book #10)
LEFT TO PREY (Book #11)
LEFT TO LURE (Book #12)
LEFT TO CRAVE (Book #13)
LEFT TO LOATHE (Book #14)
LEFT TO HARM (Book #15)

THE AU PAIR SERIES
ALMOST GONE (Book#1)
ALMOST LOST (Book #2)
ALMOST DEAD (Book #3)

ZOE PRIME MYSTERY SERIES
FACE OF DEATH (Book#1)
FACE OF MURDER (Book #2)
FACE OF FEAR (Book #3)
FACE OF MADNESS (Book #4)
FACE OF FURY (Book #5)
FACE OF DARKNESS (Book #6)

A JESSIE HUNT PSYCHOLOGICAL SUSPENSE SERIES
THE PERFECT WIFE (Book #1)
THE PERFECT BLOCK (Book #2)
THE PERFECT HOUSE (Book #3)
THE PERFECT SMILE (Book #4)
THE PERFECT LIE (Book #5)
THE PERFECT LOOK (Book #6)
THE PERFECT AFFAIR (Book #7)
THE PERFECT ALIBI (Book #8)
THE PERFECT NEIGHBOR (Book #9)
THE PERFECT DISGUISE (Book #10)
THE PERFECT SECRET (Book #11)
THE PERFECT FAÇADE (Book #12)
THE PERFECT IMPRESSION (Book #13)
THE PERFECT DECEIT (Book #14)
THE PERFECT MISTRESS (Book #15)
THE PERFECT IMAGE (Book #16)
THE PERFECT VEIL (Book #17)

ONCE HUNTED (Book #5)
ONCE PINED (Book #6)
ONCE FORSAKEN (Book #7)
ONCE COLD (Book #8)
ONCE STALKED (Book #9)
ONCE LOST (Book #10)
ONCE BURIED (Book #11)
ONCE BOUND (Book #12)
ONCE TRAPPED (Book #13)
ONCE DORMANT (Book #14)
ONCE SHUNNED (Book #15)
ONCE MISSED (Book #16)
ONCE CHOSEN (Book #17)

MACKENZIE WHITE MYSTERY SERIES
BEFORE HE KILLS (Book #1)
BEFORE HE SEES (Book #2)
BEFORE HE COVETS (Book #3)
BEFORE HE TAKES (Book #4)
BEFORE HE NEEDS (Book #5)
BEFORE HE FEELS (Book #6)
BEFORE HE SINS (Book #7)
BEFORE HE HUNTS (Book #8)
BEFORE HE PREYS (Book #9)
BEFORE HE LONGS (Book #10)
BEFORE HE LAPSES (Book #11)
BEFORE HE ENVIES (Book #12)
BEFORE HE STALKS (Book #13)
BEFORE HE HARMS (Book #14)

AVERY BLACK MYSTERY SERIES
CAUSE TO KILL (Book #1)
CAUSE TO RUN (Book #2)
CAUSE TO HIDE (Book #3)
CAUSE TO FEAR (Book #4)
CAUSE TO SAVE (Book #5)
CAUSE TO DREAD (Book #6)

KERI LOCKE MYSTERY SERIES

CHAPTER ONE

Paige stood outside the interview room, taking deep breaths to steady herself as she tried to prepare for a conversation with a serial killer.

One more conversation, one more session, and she was done. Today was the last day of her residency at the St Just Institute, and the last chance that she would have to collect data for her case study. A few weeks from now, and she would have finished writing up the case studies in her PhD thesis at Georgetown.

Today, though, she had to have one more conversation with a man who had killed… well, he'd been convicted of ten murders, but no one really knew quite how many people he'd killed. Not even her, and she'd been interviewing him for months, slowly prying information out of him, even as he tried to obfuscate and stall.

Paige needed this. She needed one more piece, one more connection.

It felt as though she had all the strands for her PhD, but they didn't quite tie together properly. She still needed that last element, that last understanding of *why* Adam Riker had chosen to kill his victims. She needed to know what had made him choose them rather than anyone else, and what had made him step over the line from a troubled man to a murderer.

Paige needed to know that, and she needed to know why he'd chosen to kill in the particular way he had, stringing his victims up like puppets while they were still alive and leaving them until they died from slow positional asphyxia. She didn't even understand why he'd tortured some and left others, just watching them until they died.

Without that understanding, her work would all feel hollow. She might have enough with her case study to get her doctorate, but it wouldn't be enough, wouldn't feel complete. *With* that information… well, with it, she might actually be able to contribute something that led to a better understanding of the criminal mind. Her work might make it easier to catch killers, or even stop them at a point before they hurt

1

anyone, by spotting the signs that they were about to step over the line and kill.

Paige carefully checked her appearance before she went in, wanting to make sure that everything was neutral, nothing would spark too much of a reaction from Adam in ways that she didn't want. Her red hair was tied back away from her slightly rounded, youthful features and green eyes, her makeup deliberately stark and simple. Paige was twenty-five, but because she was short and slightly built, she found that she had to aim for a severe look just to make people take her seriously.

Especially here, surrounded by killers. In the outside world, the wrong look or word might get a comment or two, or a disapproving expression. Here, it might cost Paige her life.

Today, she was wearing a dark suit with a skirt and a cream blouse. A ring that had been her father's sat on the smallest finger of her left hand. An enameled butterfly hairclip helped to hold her hair in place. Other than that, though, Paige wore no jewelry. Nothing that could give away too much about her.

From where she stood in front of the door, Paige could see into the interview room. Because this was a secure mental hospital rather than a normal prison, the place was decorated in calming, pastel colors of blues and greens, with soft edges to all the furniture. If Paige didn't know exactly where to look, if she hadn't been in there a hundred times before, she might not have seen the bolts keeping the table securely fastened to the floor.

Today, Adam Riker sat on one side of that table, dressed in the gray sweats that were standard wear for the hospital inmates, with his hands cuffed in front of him, secured to the table so that he wouldn't be able to lunge at Paige. He was tall and broad shouldered, in his mid-thirties, with dark hair cropped short and square jawed features that Paige guessed people found handsome. In fact, she knew that they did, because he'd been only too ready to boast about the people he'd talked into the spots he wanted them, using nothing more than the promise of those looks.

She had a harder time seeing him as handsome or attractive, because she knew all the things he'd done.

He was alone, because that was the only way he agreed to these sessions. There were guards waiting nearby, and he was cuffed to the table, but for this, it was just the two of them. He was staring her way, as if he were looking straight at Paige. There was no way that he could see her through the one-way glass of the door's window, yet those icy blue eyes were fixed on the door, staring evenly, not betraying any emotions.

Paige took another deep breath, steeling herself for the session to come. Thanks to her residency, she spent her days assessing the worst criminals, trying to diagnose those with genuine conditions, and establish which were competent to stand trial. She'd met deeply insane criminals, and evil men who were merely pretending insanity to try to avoid paying for their crimes. With all of them, there was a small thread of fear that went alongside her fascination.

Somehow though, stepping into this room was harder than her conversations with any of the others.

Paige made herself do it though, stepping inside while trying to hide the note of disquiet she always felt while approaching Riker behind a mask of friendly professionalism. She made herself smile Adam's way. He always told her more when she smiled.

"Paige, so good to see you again," he said, as if he were Prof. Thornton, her tutor back in Georgetown, and not a killer sitting in handcuffs. "Please, sit down."

Paige knew that for the psychological game it was. If she sat, she was doing what he wanted. If she didn't, then she was reacting to him out of fear. Either way, he won, exactly the way he wanted. Adam liked to win.

The only thing to do was to ignore the game completely, and sit anyway, since it was what Paige had been planning to do all along. The first thing Paige did was to take out a small recording device and set it on the table, halfway between the two of them. She set it running, making sure that it was working before she continued. It was easier than trying to take notes, and safer, too. It meant that she could keep her eyes on him at all times.

"How are you feeling today, Adam?" Paige asked, being careful to betray none of the unease that she felt.

She saw him cock his head to one side, almost mockingly. "Are we really still discussing feelings, Paige? Very well, today, I'm feeling quite happy. There, does that satisfy you?"

"*Can* you feel happiness?" Paige asked, more interested in that than the answer to her first question.

It should have been a simple question, but there was nothing simple when it came to a man like this. It was one of the reasons why she'd come back to talk to him again and again. She'd started her thesis thinking that it would involve case studies on a dozen different killers, but instead, Adam Riker had come to fill it.

The serial killer smiled faintly at that question. "Do I feel it the way you do, you mean? How would I know, Paige? How would I know what you feel?"

"Empathy, perhaps?" Paige suggested, leaning in very slightly as she said the words. Even so, she was careful about the distance between them, judging just how far he could reach in his cuffs.

Adam gave her a disappointed look. "Empathy? Remind me of my diagnosis, please."

"Anti-social personality disorder, scoring highly on Hare's psychopathy scale." It wasn't as if Paige was likely to forget any of that. She'd been over his notes enough times. The only reason that she didn't simply call him a psychopath and have done with it was that the American Psychological Association didn't formally recognize it as a diagnosis.

"One of the defining qualities of which is a *lack* of empathy," Adam pointed out, bringing his hands together and steepling his fingers. "Although I have always considered it a lie in any case."

"What do you think is a lie?" Paige asked.

"Empathy. I am supposed to look at you and know how you might feel, feel what you feel, but honestly, what does any of us get except a reflection of our own thoughts and feelings?"

This was what it could be like, sometimes, with Adam. Him challenging her the way Prof. Thornton might have, treating her more like a student to bring on than the psychiatrist there to work with him. As if he could help to mold her and shape her into something more.

Paige decided to follow the thread at least a little way. Sometimes, it was better to go along with Adam, to let him talk about what he wanted.

"And do you not think that the things I think and feel might be similar to the ones you do? That another person might not feel the same way?"

This look was as cold as the icy depths of a lake, all warmth and humanity draining out of Adam's face, in a reminder that both were little more than an act to him. A reminder of exactly what he was, underneath. Paige felt her heart beating faster at the sight of it, the urge to get up from her chair and run for the door almost overwhelming, in spite of the knowledge that she should be perfectly safe with Adam restrained.

4

It was a look that reminded Paige of all the violence Adam Riker was capable of, the men and women who had been found bound and tortured, left to die. Of the two inmates he had killed in his time here, when they'd tried to attack him. It was a look that made her want to shrink back.

"There is *no one* else like me," Adam said.

Paige decided to placate him. "That's true. You're very special, Adam. It's why I'm focusing so much of my research on you."

Just like that, the coldness drifted away, replaced once again by a warm, almost friendly, smile. The speed of the change was almost as disconcerting as the empty hostility that had preceded it.

"Although I must say, I feel a particular connection towards you, Paige."

"That's… very flattering," Paige managed, even though it was just about the most disconcerting thing she could hear from a serial killer. "Does that connection extend to helping me with my research today?"

"Yes, your research," he said. "What do you have for me this time, Paige? A few more Likert scales to test my responses? Perhaps you'd like to talk about my family again? My abusive father and uncle. My absent mother? Maybe you'd like to know where I see myself on the whole 'primary, secondary, egocentric, charismatic, distempered' psychopath spectrum? Where have *you* placed my particular neurocognitive peculiarities, incidentally, Paige?"

Neurocognitive peculiarities. That was an almost banal way of describing his lack of empathy, high charisma, and urge to kill. It made it all sound like a minor eccentricity, rather than something that had cost men and women their lives.

"It's… complicated," Paige replied, determined not to be fazed by his sudden descent into the academic terminology. Nobody, least of all her, had ever suggested that Adam Riker was unintelligent.

If anything, he was quite the opposite. He was intelligent, charming, capable of considerable forethought. He seemed to have seduced at least half of his victims into letting him start to tie them, while with the others, he had planned every step of his killings with painstaking effort.

He also had no regard for anything beyond his self-interest and had aberrant impulses that led him to kill again and again.

"Complicated?" Adam said. Again, Paige saw a subtle tilt of his head that might have indicated disapproval. "Is *that* what you'll say in your thesis? I think the panel for your defense of it will want more than

5

that. At least take a position on primary versus secondary. Was I born this way, or was I made? I take it you're still wedded to Grey's neurocognitive model of Behavioral Inhibition Systems?"

Paige knew better than to play this game with him by trying to defend her thesis when he had no interest in being convinced. This was just Adam trying to pick at her in the easiest way he could, by trying to undermine her confidence in her work.

"We're here to talk about you, Adam," Paige pointed out, in her most professional tone. She paused for a moment or two. "And this might be your last chance to talk to me. This is going to be our final session."

Paige watched for a flicker of response. Did that make him angry, sad, disappointed, happy? It was impossible to tell for sure, with Adam.

"Our final session?" Adam said. He sounded almost surprised by the announcement. "You're almost done, then."

Paige nodded. "So is there anything else that you want to talk to me about? Is there anything that has come up in our sessions that you want to clarify or go over?"

"Are there any last juicy morsels that I can drop for you to incorporate?" Adam suggested. "I think you have enough for a thesis. I think you've had enough for a month or more, and yet you've kept coming back, Paige? Why is that? Is it because you feel some kind of connection between us?"

He clearly wasn't feeling in a cooperative mood today. Some days, he liked to talk and talk. Others, he played games like this.

Paige tried for flattery again. It seemed to be something Adam responded to. He was so certain of his own brilliance, after all, and he seemed to like having that reinforced by others.

"Perhaps I just find your story interesting."

"Oh, it's very interesting. A veritable study in psychopathy: a view on a psychopathic patient with case notes."

Paige froze in place as he said those words. They were, word for word, the title of a paper she'd published following a conference three months ago. She felt her mouth fall open in shock.

"How-"

"Oh, did you think you let nothing slip in our little sessions?" Adam asked, leaning back in his chair as far as his cuffed hands would allow him. The intense look of a serial killer was back on his face then, either because he wanted to scare her, or because he simply didn't care about

6

hiding anymore. "Did you think that I wasn't paying *attention*? Did you think I wouldn't find anything else out?"

The warmth had faded out of him completely, so that he seemed to be reciting almost robotically.

"Paige King, twenty-five. Your father was Swedish, your mother is from Virginia, where your family lived. You were an only child. You had a very happy childhood, until you were ten. Very sweet and bucolic."

"Stop this," Paige insisted, as she started to realize where Adam was going with this. He'd played games before, but he'd never attacked her like this. He'd never shown before that he knew the one thing about Paige that she least wanted other people to know.

He ignored her and kept going. "What was it like, when you found him dead in the woods? When you found the body, so carefully exsanguinated. The way the others had been. When you realized that he'd been killed by... well, someone like me."

Paige had to fight back tears, caught between her shock, grief, and anger. In that moment, she was standing over her father's corpse again, the horror of it all-consuming.

"You know nothing about me," she snapped, trying to force him back from the verbal grip he currently seemed to have on her.

"I know *everything* about you," Adam replied. "You gave me so many snippets when you tried to get me to talk to you, Paige. Did you think I wouldn't remember? I know your mother waited precisely three years before she remarried. I know what kind of man she married. I know about the abuse, Paige. I know what he did to you. I'm so sorry."

Those three words were like the cut of a scalpel, catching Paige completely by surprise. There were some things she *didn't* talk about. She'd barely discussed them even with Prof. Thornton.

Adam didn't stop, though. "Whereas what do you really know about me? You've spent your time studying psychopaths, but you can sit here in front of me and expect me not to be as smart as you? As capable? Tell me, is that ring you wear your father's? Tell me that, and I'll tell you why I did it all. I'll tell you *everything*."

He made it sound so simple, offering everything Paige had wanted when she came into the room, but she knew then that it would be a deal with the devil. Paige recoiled from the table in shock at the onslaught of words. She'd thought she was so careful to give nothing about herself away, and yet here was a killer with all the details of the tragedy that hurt her most.

7

Paige had to force herself not to show any emotion. Had to force herself to just stand calmly and take her recorder, switching it off crisply.

"Leaving so soon?" Adam asked.

Paige forced her face into a mask, tried to show no emotions at all. "You said it yourself, I already have everything I need. I don't have to stay here to listen to you, and I'm never coming back to see you again. I don't need you anymore, Adam."

She ignored the part where she didn't have *everything*. She still didn't have that last part that would tie her thesis together. She would be left with a hole that she just had to hope the thesis committee wouldn't notice.

Right then, she didn't show any of that. It was the only way she had to hurt him, when he wanted her attention so much. Right then, she *wanted* to hurt him. The way he'd just hurt her.

Instead, he laughed.

"I think we'll see each other soon enough. Now that our sessions are done, I think it's time for me to leave."

That was enough to stop Paige's movement towards the door for a moment.

"Leave."

"Escape, if you prefer," Adam said. He said it so calmly, as if it were a simple fact. "I'm going to, very soon."

Paige stared at him in disbelief. "Why are you telling me this? What game are you playing?"

She understood that part of Adam Riker, at least. He liked to play games. He liked to prove that he was the clever one, and that everyone around him was stupid by comparison. Well, Paige wasn't going to give him the satisfaction.

He shrugged. "I'm telling you so that you'll try to stop me. And you'll fail. There's *nothing* you can do to stop me, Paige."

Paige had heard enough. She stalked from the room, trying not to let Adam see how much this had gotten under her skin. The last thing she heard was Adam's voice calling after her.

"Maybe once I'm out, we'll talk again. On my terms. I have plans for you, Paige."

*

8

Paige rushed to the warden's office, having to force herself to walk rather than run. Running would have been a kind of admission of defeat, a victory for Adam Riker even if he couldn't see it.

So she walked past the rooms that held the patients there, each one as secure as a prison cell. She walked past a small group on their way to a group session, watched over by a couple of guards who never took their eyes from them for a second. She passed through a secure door using her code, then walked up a flight of stairs to get to the warden's office.

Dr. Neil was in there, giving some paperwork his full attention. He was an older man who always wore sharp suits, and kept his white hair slicked back. His features were slightly squashed looking, but his eyes darted around with intelligence. He managed a smile as Paige entered.

He obviously couldn't see how worried she was right then.

"Ah, Paige. All done on your last day with us?"

Paige nodded. She was done. After some of the things Adam had just said, she would be glad if she didn't see this place again. She certainly never wanted to see *him*.

"I also wanted to tell you something that came up in my last session with Adam Riker. He... he told me that he plans to escape."

Dr. Neil didn't look as worried by that as Paige felt. Perhaps because he hadn't seen the look on the killer's face while he'd said it. The cold certainty, as if he were already guaranteed his freedom, and everything along the way was just an inconvenient detail.

"Many of the patients here fantasize about such things, but they are sent here for a reason," Dr. Neil pointed out, in a voice that seemed far too even and reasonable to Paige. "This is a *secure* institution. We do not have escapes."

"Even so, I think he was serious about making the attempt," Paige said. She needed to make sure that the warden understood just how dangerous this could be. "He... made threats. Towards me, and my family."

A look of sympathy crossed Dr. Neil's face as Paige said that. "I still don't think that anything is actually going to happen, Paige. If Adam Riker, or anyone else, could escape from here, they would have, by now."

"Dr. Neil, I've spent months now having sessions with Riker, and I'm telling you that he wasn't making an empty threat." Paige could feel the tension running through her body just at the thought of it.

9

"Even if he just makes the attempt, people could get hurt in the process."

She saw Dr. Neil considering that, head bobbing slightly as if weighing up each possibility was enough to move it.

"I trust your opinion, Paige," he said at last. "I wouldn't have you running assessments on new arrivals if I didn't. Do you honestly believe that Adam Riker is that dangerous? That he will actually try to do what he's said?"

Paige didn't hesitate to nod. "That, and a lot more. I've met a lot of dangerous people here, and of all of them, he... he scares me."

Admitting that was hard, because Paige didn't want to admit the kind of power Adam had over her by making her afraid, but at least it was enough to get Dr. Neil's attention.

"Look, if you're that worried, I'll increase the number of guards near his room for the next few days. Just until he gets the message that whatever plan he has won't work. Just remember, you get to go home now, and he doesn't get to go anywhere."

"Strictly speaking, I'm going to dinner at Professor Thornton's house," Paige said.

"A celebration for the end of your thesis?"

Paige nodded.

"Then celebrate," Dr. Neil said. "You get to enjoy yourself. You get the joy of this all being done. Adam gets to sit in his cell. You won't have to see his face again."

Paige hoped so; she really did.

CHAPTER TWO

Adam waited as patiently as he could in the cell they called a hospital room, perfectly still, staring at the blankness of the walls, listening to the sounds of the guards stomping their way around the corridors as the prisoners slept.

There were more of them wandering the halls, just as he'd hoped. Enough that it would confuse things. Paige had done exactly what he wanted.

He generally found that people did, one way or another. Even when they thought that they couldn't be manipulated. *Especially* when they thought that they couldn't be manipulated. They all had their little levers that made them act or fail to act. For some, it was money, for others, fear, for a few, the promise of love or power, the sense that they were in control of the situation.

Adam told them what they needed to hear, and they danced for him like puppets on a string. It made the moments when he actually strung them up like puppets all the more meaningful. More meaningful than any of them were, at least. They were ants, compared to him.

Although he had to admit that Paige was... special.

Take the guard who would even now be approaching his cell. What had it taken to persuade him? A little charm. The promise of sex, obviously. Lesser people seemed to put so much emphasis on that, as if it weren't something that could be gotten anywhere, anytime.

There was money in addition to the sex, of course. Julio was a bad gambler, and Adam had called in some favors to arrange for him to run into much better ones, with the result that he owed more than he could ever afford to repay. The kind of debt that got people scared and stupid. Julio had already paid off a part of those debts, with the promise of much more to come when he helped with this.

He'd arranged it all carefully, all leading up to this point. To the moment when he would leave this place behind and do everything he had to do next.

Julio knocked on the door first to announce his presence, almost delicately. So polite. Then he opened it, revealing himself there, standing shorter than Adam but broader, muscles filling out his

11

uniform. He was unshaven and heavy browed, with broad features and dark hair. He was carrying a bag. Adam could see the look on his face of... hope? Expectation? He'd worked hard at learning to read faces, at least partly so that he could make his own show whatever he wanted. Whatever people expected.

Right now, he made it show delight that Julio had come here to save him. As if he were some kind of damsel in distress, needing to be rescued.

"You came," Adam said. "I wasn't sure if you would."

He added that little hint of doubt deliberately. Julio was a man who tended to rise to the bait with things like that, far too easy to provoke. It was a part of what made him such a bad gambler, and such a useful helper in this tonight.

"Of course I came!" Julio said, starting forward towards Adam as if he might embrace him.

Adam put a coy hand on his chest. "If we start here, we won't stop, and then all the extra guards will catch us as they come by."

That brought a flicker of disappointment, and Adam assuaged it by moving his hand to the guard's cheek in a caress. It seemed like the least he could get away with doing.

"We have all the time in the world. I have a place waiting for us, and it's far more comfortable than this."

The disappointment quickly changed to eagerness. Adam never ceased to be disappointed by how easy to manipulate people were. They were all so *weak*.

Take Paige King. There had been a point in their sessions where Adam had started to believe that she might be almost as clever as him. He still held out hopes for her. Yet she'd let him find out all about her easily, and she'd given him exactly what he wanted now. He wasn't sure whether to kill her, or... no, better not to get ahead of himself.

"Do you have it?" Adam asked Julio, wanting to focus on tonight.

He saw Julio bring out a bundle of clothes from the bag. A uniform of black pants and brown shirt exactly matching the one Julio wore. Boots, a belt. An ID card, even if the photograph on it wasn't of Adam. And a cap, so that his face wouldn't be quite so obvious.

"Are you sure this will work?" Julio asked as Adam started to change into the uniform. He saw Julio's eyes roving over him and suppressed a flash of annoyance at the intrusion. "There are a lot of guards around now. And they'll be watching CCTV in the halls."

12

"More guards are good," Adam replied. "More guards are the *point*."

It was why he'd pushed Paige in their session. Well, one of the reasons, anyway. It was always better to accomplish more than one thing.

Adam finished dressing. "How do I look?"

"Wonderful, of course," Julio began.

Adam waved that off with another flicker of irritation. "Do I look enough like a guard to pass for one?"

Julio nodded, and he looked serious enough while he did it that Adam was prepared to accept it as true, rather than as mere flattery. He straightened up, picturing how the guards walked, with that heavy tread and hint of swagger that came from knowing they were the ones in charge. That was almost as important as the disguise.

It was so easy to become someone else, when he'd had to work to show the slightest emotion growing up, when everything that showed on his face was an act, and when failing to do so had gotten him beaten. It was one act he'd perfected to the extent that he could fool almost anyone, and here, now, it was going to be more than enough to fool a few guards.

He and Julio stepped out into the blank, institutional expanse of the corridor, shutting the door behind them and walking without hurry. Running would be the worst mistake they could make, drawing far too much attention. Adam had no problem with staying cool as they moved along past the other cells. Fear was for other people. His only real concern was that Julio might not be so cool. Already, he could see the guard looking around as if he expected discovery at any moment.

"Stay calm," Adam said. "People will only spot us if they think we are behaving unusually. You can do this, Julio."

He pitched his voice with a note of encouragement, when he would much rather have snapped at the guard for being so foolish.

The two of them kept walking without hurry. The corridors were lined with artworks that were meant to be soothing, mixed in with others that had been painted by the inmates in art therapy classes. Most of those inmates would be asleep in their cells, and the few who looked out through their doors gave no signs of recognizing him.

Adam saw more guards walking the corridors. A pair of them even turned their way. Adam pulled his cap down and kept moving towards them, making sure that he didn't give any sign of hesitation.

Adam didn't have the kind of doubts that other people might have had in his position: what if the guards recognized his face? What if they saw that, while he had the uniform, he didn't have the full belt of cuffs, nightstick, and stun gun with which to subdue violent prisoners? What if Julio got second thoughts and simply denounced him? People could be used, but they could rarely be trusted.

Adam wasn't prey to those doubts. Instead, he continued walking, reminding himself that the whole point of ensuring that there were more guards on duty was to make sure that there were plenty from other wings. Plenty of unfamiliar faces.

"How are things your way?" one of them asked.

"All quiet," Adam replied, because he wasn't about to let Julio do the talking on this.

The other one looked at him for a moment or two. "Don't think I've seen you on this wing before."

Adam felt sure for a second there that he'd been found out, and that his whole scheme would come to a crashing halt. He felt himself tensing to fight, ready to lunge forward. Even so, he forced out the next words.

"I usually work on B wing. I'm only over here because *apparently* one of the prisoners threatened to escape. Like they don't do that every couple of days."

That got a short laugh from one of the guards there. "Apparently, one of the shrinks got spooked. Tell me, you were back that way. Did Riker escape yet?"

"Not yet," Adam replied, making another joke of it. It got a bigger laugh than the last comment. "But we'd better keep moving, just in case."

He nodded again to the guards and kept walking, with Julio beside him. The guard looked flustered as they both headed off, away from the danger.

"That was too close," Julio said. "They could have-"

"They didn't." Adam couldn't keep the annoyance out of his voice for a second. "We need to keep moving. If we stop, then they *will* catch us, and... well, I'm already in a cell. You're the one who stands to lose his freedom."

Sometimes, threats worked better than enticements. In this case, it was enough to keep Julio moving, all the way to a door with a keypad lock.

14

Adam stood back to let him punch in the numbers. A light flashed green, and the door swung open. They stepped through, out of the area that held the inmates, and into the sections reserved for administration.

Here, there was even less reason for anyone to look their way. Adam had worked out a long time ago that people saw what they wanted to see. They saw a handsome face, a winning smile, and they assumed that everything was all right. Here, it was even simpler. Inmates were in the sections reserved for inmates. In their cells. Adam wasn't there, and therefore, he couldn't be an inmate. It was the kind of circular logic that made his life considerably easier, even as he despised people for it.

He actually smiled at one of the nurses on duty, seated at a desk, a small selection of medical supplies set out in front of her. She was pretty enough, in her way, and he found himself leaning over the desk to speak to her.

"How's your evening going?" he asked.

"Well enough," she replied. "No one needing medical attention, no sedatives to calm anyone."

Adam had been given more than his share of those, in his time there. They'd fogged his brain, slowed his body. "Well, that's good. Gives you more time to talk to-"

Julio chose that moment to cough, pointedly. "We have things to do."

Trust him to get jealous. But then, Adam had expected that. He was already moving back away from the desk. As he did so, he kept the small surgical scalpel he'd picked up hidden in his hand. It was better to be armed.

They made their way through the admin area to one of the smaller exits, used for bringing in the supplies that a place like this needed to run. There was another door, with another code needed to open it. There was also a guard, and Adam found his grip tightening on the scalpel.

This time, though, it was Julio who came to the rescue. "Oh, hey, Kevin. Hell of a night to have to double up."

"Tell me about it."

"Can you punch us out? Apparently, this whole increased security thing means that we have to walk the perimeter every hour."

The guard on the door frowned. "That's not the usual pattern."

"I think that's the point," Adam said. "Do something that anyone trying to escape can't have planned for ahead of time."

He tensed as he moved closer, ready to strike if this last guard gave any hint that he wasn't going to go along with it.

Then the guard shrugged. "It all seems like a lot of trouble over nothing to me, but I guess I'm not the one out walking in the rain. Out you go."

He opened the door for them and stood back to let them go. Again, Adam forced himself to walk normally, making his way out with Julio and pacing around in the direction of the institution's parking lot.

"Have your keys ready," Adam said. "It's only a matter of time before they raise an alarm."

Julio nodded, getting out the key to his car and holding them ready in his hand. They both kept moving towards the parking lot, still not running yet, because there was a chance that someone might be watching, even now. At this time of night, the parking lot was almost empty. Only a few cars sat there, belonging to the staff, with large spaces in between.

"We did it," Julio said, with obvious joy. He turned to Adam as if he might kiss him. "We actually-"

That was when Adam slashed his stolen scalpel across Julio's throat, fast as a striking snake. He stepped aside as blood spurted from the wound, not wanting to get sprayed by it. The guard's hands went up to his throat, as if he could keep the blood inside his body that way. Shock and pain filled his face, followed by a hurt expression, presumably as he realized just how he'd been used.

"I wish I had enough time to do this properly," Adam said, clutching Julio to him and stabbing him twice more for good measure. This *wasn't* the way he preferred to kill. "But I'm in kind of a hurry, and honestly, I never found you that interesting."

At least he could hurt Julio a little more that way. Adam kept a strong grip on him, holding him as close as a lover might have. He watched until the life left Julio's eyes, watching for that split second that represented the shift from a live person to a dead thing.

Adam lowered Julio to the ground. He reached down to take his key fob and clicked it, watching for the lights that told him which car to take. He also took the time to take Julio's cuffs and stun gun. Both might come in useful soon enough. Abandoning the body, Adam made his way over to the car, a beaten-up BMW, and got inside.

He started to drive off, moving quickly now, because it was only a matter of time before his escape was discovered. Adam regretted that rush. He hated other people forcing his hand like that. He liked to be the one who decided what happened, and when.

He'd had to kill Julio quickly. There hadn't been time for more. But where he was going next, there would be *plenty* of time. He'd make sure of it.

CHAPTER THREE

By the time Agent Christopher Marriott of the FBI's Behavioral Analysis Unit arrived at St Just's, it was already awash with blue lights, a sea of police swarming the place as they searched the surrounding area for any sign of Adam Riker.

Christopher could have told them that they were wasting their time. If one of the facility's killers had a plan good enough to get him out of the building, they weren't going to find him anywhere nearby. He wasn't going to break out, and then sit there waiting in the surrounding bushes for someone to find him.

He pulled up in his Pontiac and unfolded his six-foot-four frame from the driver's seat, stretching out as he surveyed the surrounding police, trying to work out who was in charge there. He pulled his FBI issue jacket tighter around his broad shoulders and pulled a cap down over his sandy hair against the cold of the night.

He strode over to the spot where police tape cordoned off a space in the parking lot, because that appeared to be the current focal point of attention. A forensic team was working there already, with a couple of uniformed cops making sure that no one breached the perimeter of the tape. They were needed, because somehow, there were already camera crews and reporters out there, all pushing to get the closest view of what was happening. News of the escape had traveled fast.

"Can you tell us what's going on, Agent?" a female reporter asked, and then looked closer at him, as if just noticing his square jaw and boyish good looks for the first time. "Maybe we can get an interview with you on camera. I'm sure it will love you."

And Christopher was sure that he would hate every moment of it. He definitely had no interest in taking the time to do so. His bosses had told him plenty of times that he needed to try being nicer to the press, but Christopher had never been that good at listening to his superiors. Only his impressive clean up rate kept them from transferring him out of the BAU completely. It was certainly the only part that mattered to him.

Still, he'd learned a few stock phrases to say at times like this.

"Details will be released in due course," Christopher said, stepping past the reporter without stopping. There were more of the reporters in the way, but he timed the moment a gap opened up between them like a quarterback making a run and managed to slip through without one of them managing to get a question off.

He wasn't surprised to see a couple of US marshals there among the police, apparently directing things. Manhunts were what they did best, after all. In this case, though, they were going to need him, and the particular expertise that the BAU could bring to the table.

"What's the FBI doing here?" one of them asked. He was a short man at least ten years older than Christopher's thirty-two, with a barrel chest and a thinning hairline; he didn't look entirely happy to see Christopher there.

"Agent Marriott, BAU. Since there's now a serial killer on the loose, that makes it my department's responsibility."

Just saying the words brought with them a thread of worry for Christopher at the thought of Adam Riker being out there. Tonight, a man was on the loose who should never have seen daylight again, a man who represented the worst of the worst, and whose freedom meant that no one would be safe until he was caught again.

The pressure of being the one who had to catch Riker was there on Christopher's shoulders almost from the moment that he thought it. At the same time, though, he could feel the rising excitement of the chase. Men like Adam Riker were the reason why he'd joined the BAU in the first place.

"Are you going to get in our way?" the marshal asked, obviously assuming that the involvement of the BAU would only complicate his efforts.

Christopher was already shaking his head, though. He'd encountered this kind of resistance before. "You do your thing. I'm not going to argue when you're the best ones for a full-scale man hunt. Set up roadblocks, scour the places he might have gone, but when he avoids all of that-"

"He won't."

There was a certainty to the words that Christopher found completely misplaced. He kept going.

"When he does, that's where I come in. Now, what exactly happened here? How did he escape from the facility?"

The marshal didn't look happy about it, but at least he answered the question. "He had help. The facility's cameras have him walking out with this guard." He gestured to the body lying there, still being worked on by the forensic team. "Somehow, he persuaded this guard to break him out. Why would anyone even do anything like that?"

"Money, threats, promises," Christopher said. "To understand exactly what combination, I'd have to know more about the guard. From his file, Riker is highly manipulative."

He was the kind of man who could persuade almost anyone to do what he wanted; he had manipulated many of his victims into positions they couldn't escape from.

"Is that the kind of high-level analysis they teach you at Quantico?" the marshal scoffed.

Christopher ignored him. He'd run into plenty of people who felt that the BAU was nonsense, not real investigative work. Besides, he guessed that the other man was picking a fight because he was worried. He had to know as well as Christopher did that they were playing catch up with a serial killer at this point.

"Where's the head of the facility?" Christopher asked. If he was going to get ahead of Riker, then he needed to get some kind of insight into the serial killer's mind.

"That would be Dr. Neil." The marshal gestured to a spot where a white haired, older civilian in a sharp suit was standing in the parking lot, watching proceedings with a worried expression.

Christopher went over to the man. This close, he looked tired, and very slightly bedraggled around the edges, with uncombed hair, and one cuff of his shirt not quite fastened correctly. Christopher had the impression that he'd come out in a rush, probably after a panicked phone call from the facility to let him know that Riker had escaped.

"Dr. Neil?" he said. "I'm Agent Marriott, with the FBI's behavioral analysis unit."

"The FBI?" Christopher saw Dr. Neil's eyes widen slightly at the announcement, but then the older man nodded as he started to understand. "Yes, of course you're here. I don't know what to tell you, though, Agent. I only just got here myself. I got a call when I was at home."

"But presumably you've already gathered some information about what's going on?" Christopher said. He couldn't imagine the head of the facility rushing here and then not asking his staff what was happening. They would probably tell him things in the immediate aftermath that might take hours for the police to get out of anyone.

"I know that a prisoner, Adam Riker, escaped. That's bad enough, but what's worse is that he made a mockery of our security precautions. He managed to break out even after he came out and told a member of my staff that he was going to."

Christopher tried to make some kind of sense of that. "He actually told one of your people that he was planning to escape? And this person reported it?"

He saw the doctor nod and saw the embarrassment there in the man's expression. "Paige came straight to my office to do so after her session with Riker."

"Session? What session?" Christopher tried to wind things back a little. He needed to catch up with what was going on. "Who is this 'Paige,' and why was she meeting with Adam Riker?"

Dr. Neil took a second or two before answering. He was obviously nervous, and had the sense that Christopher was making some kind of criticism of the way he ran his facility.

"Paige King is a resident here, or was. Today was her last day. She has been doing a PhD on criminal psychology."

"A grad student?" Christopher asked. "Is that usual?"

"We had her perform evaluations here, and she also undertook psychological interviews with many of the patients. She had regular sessions with Adam Riker. I understand that his case had started to form one of the main case studies for her thesis."

"So she knew Riker well?"

"If you think that she played any role in all of this, I should remind you that she was the one who told me about his threat to escape. I doubled the number of guards on that wing because of that threat."

Christopher hadn't been thinking that, although it would be easy to get suspicious. The presence of increased numbers of guards seemed to have helped Riker's escape, not hindered it. He'd also escaped right on the day when this 'Paige King' had finished her work.

Yet somehow, those suspicions didn't add up to her being a suspect in Christopher's mind.

A grad student psychologist didn't represent a way out to an inmate like Riker. She couldn't walk him out of the building. That was obviously why he'd used a guard instead. And he didn't need to bring her in on any kind of plot to get her to increase the number of guards. He just needed to make his threat.

The fact that he'd done it *today* was more interesting, though. He'd picked the day when this woman had left and wouldn't be speaking to him anymore. To Christopher, that said that Riker perceived some kind of connection between himself and this woman. When it came to a serial killer, that was anything but a good thing.

She might even be a target for him. He might be heading there right now.

At the same time, she was someone out there who had spent time interviewing Riker, studying him. Someone who probably knew the way his mind worked better than anyone else. In other words, exactly the kind of person Christopher needed if he was going to find Riker.

"Where can I find Paige King?" Christopher asked. "I need to talk to her."

"She isn't here," Dr. Neil said. "As I said, she finished her residency today. I think she said she was planning to go visit her thesis supervisor for dinner."

Christopher could have done this in the morning, but with a man on the run, and with the possibility that Riker might choose her as his next target, there was no time to spare.

Yes, there were other things that he could do, but most of those things were ones that the marshals or the local police could do easily without his help. He was there from the BAU, and as far as Christopher was concerned, knowing more about how Adam Riker was thinking was the best way to catch him.

"I need to know her supervisor's name, right now."

*

Paige took the time to get changed when she got home, so that she now wore a green sweater and jeans rather than her work clothes. Prof. Thornton might be her doctoral supervisor, but he wasn't one for formality. He would probably think that something was strange if she showed up in her suit. She dug around in her refrigerator until she found an unopened bottle of wine of indeterminate quality, then called an Uber to take her over to the Thorntons' place.

It took Paige up towards the suburbs, into the kind of quiet neighborhood that Paige had really only seen on TV until she'd gotten here. The town she'd grown up in was much more... bucolic than the big city, both tiny and far more sprawling than these ordered rows of identically built family properties, with their white picket fences and their driveways for the two-family cars.

"Are you off to a party?" the driver asked her as she got in.

"To dinner. Celebrating the end of my PhD." Even as she said it, Paige knew what the next question was going to be.

"A PhD? Impressive. What's it about?"

That was the same question everyone asked Paige at this point, and she'd learned a long time ago that trying to go into the full details of it all just met with blank looks. Even people in the same general field didn't quite get it, most of the time. Instead, she'd come up with the elevator pitch version of it.

"I study psychopaths, specifically serial killers, trying to work out what makes them who they are."

"Why would you want to know that?" the driver asked.

Why, always why at this point. Paige had her answer to that question ready, as well, as carefully pre-prepared as if she'd been defending her thesis in front of a committee.

"Because if we know that, we might be able to do something to change it and make the world safer. It might also make it easier to catch the ones who commit crimes."

They were both good, safe reasons. Reasons that people would understand. Reasons that made the average person listening understand that, as esoteric as her field sounded, it had potentially direct benefits for the world. Both of those reasons were also lies.

There was one reason that Paige wanted to know all about serial killers: to understand why one of their number had taken her father from her.

Maybe even to track them down, one day.

The thought of that was even more uncomfortable than usual, coming so soon after Adam Riker had reminded her of it, had thrown the fact at her like a weapon. Paige found herself running her hand over the ring she wore, a brief memory of her father laughing in the sun flashing through her mind. He had always been quick to laugh, seeming big and strong enough that the world couldn't touch him, and nothing could hurt either of them while he was there.

How wrong she'd been.

She could still remember standing over his body in the woods, looking down at it lying so pale and empty of blood. Paige remembered confusion, and horror. She remembered standing there for what felt like hours, just staring.

Paige could only sit there and think about her father until the Thorntons' place came into view. It was large and timber framed, older than most of the neighborhood around it, although the Thorntons had remodeled it until it seemed to fit them like a glove. She got out and hurried to the door, heading for the safety of company, rather than the danger of being left with her own thoughts, making sure to manage a smile as she rang the bell to the large, timber framed family home.

Haley Thornton was the one who answered the door. She was in her fifties, as short as Paige was, but plump and round faced, in a way that served to make her look almost perpetually cheerful. Her short blonde hair was currently spiked, and she wore a particularly impressive collection of earrings through both ears, all of which contrasted sharply with the understatement of her usual slacks and t shirt combination.

She hugged Paige, just about the only person who did at the moment, if she didn't count the awkward hugs that came when she went back to Virginia to visit her mother every year. Haley took the wine from her, smiling at it as if it were some great vintage Paige had brought and not just whatever had been cheapest last time she'd been shopping. The Thorntons knew about wine. One of their bedrooms had even been converted into a kind of makeshift wine cellar, with racks around the walls.

"Come in, come in. Francis is in the kitchen. You know what he gets like when he starts cooking."

Paige knew, and it was probably strange that she knew that about her thesis supervisor, but it didn't feel that way to her.

Haley led the way through the house, although Paige knew it perfectly by now. It had been a shock, the first time she'd found herself invited to her doctoral supervisor's home, but now she'd been there so many times that it felt almost as familiar as her apartment. She was as likely to have a meeting about her thesis here as at the university, because Prof. Thornton spent plenty of time working from home these days.

The kitchen was large enough that it could have served an entire restaurant, a vision in stainless steel work surfaces. Prof. Thornton stood at the heart of it all, wearing tweed pants, a cream shirt, and an apron. He was much taller than both his wife and Paige, with a short, dark beard that had acquired a lot more gray hairs since Paige started her doctorate. It was hard to believe sometimes that this was one of the most respected psychology professors teaching out of Georgetown.

"I'm making steak Dianne," the professor announced, "with chocolate souffle to follow. We're celebrating, after all."

24

He gestured to a large dining table that took up half the kitchen, solid and made of dark oak. Paige took a seat gratefully, happy to just forget for a moment or two.

"How does it feel to have finished your residency?" Prof. Thornton asked.

"It's…," Paige hadn't paused long enough to really process it all. "A relief, I guess."

"But?"

Of course he saw that there was a but. A professor of criminal psychology wasn't about to miss anything as obvious as that. Their tutorials were halfway to being therapy sessions, most of the time.

"But there are all the uncertainties of what I do next," Paige said. "And we don't even know that my thesis will be accepted."

"Of course it will be," Prof. Thornton said. He flashed a smile. "You have a brilliant supervisor, for one thing."

Haley snorted. Quite a lot of their relationship seemed to consist of her poking holes in her husband's attempts at grandeur. "And modest, with it. But on one part, I'm inclined to agree with Francis: you've done all the work. Your thesis is ready. Maybe you have to make a few minor corrections, but other than that? Soon, it will be Doctor Paige King, PhD."

The thought of that brought a thrill of excitement with it, because it was everything that Paige had been working towards for years now, but also did nothing to get rid of any of the fears she had about what might come next for her.

"It's still a lot to process," Paige said. She'd come to the end of years of work, and just like that, it was done.

"Well, maybe take some time to do that," Prof. Thornton suggested as he brought over food. "Relax a little. Maybe take the time to catch up with your family."

"I thought you said relax," Paige replied.

There was nothing relaxing about visits to her mother. She couldn't understand why her daughter would want to study serial killers after her husband had been killed by one.

She never mentioned the things her new husband had done, either. It was just a wall of silence between the two of them, impossible to breach.

"Maybe now's a good time to get back in touch." Prof. Thornton lifted his glass. "Here's to the end of your residency, and new beginnings."

"New beginnings," Paige repeated, clinking glasses. A new career, where she wouldn't have to spend her day sitting across from a serial killer if she didn't choose to.

Of course, there was the possibility that she *might* choose to, or at least that she might continue to study them. She still needed answers, still wanted to understand the man who had taken her father from her. For now, though, maybe it would be best to take a short break.

That was the moment when someone started hammering on the door. Prof. Thornton got up to answer it, but Paige found herself going with him, wanting to see what the fuss was all about.

A tall man in an FBI jacket stood on the doorstep, ID held out in front of him so that it was almost the first thing that Paige noticed. The second thing that she noticed was that he was attractive, probably in his thirties, with sandy hair and square jawed features. If Paige had met him in a bar somewhere, she would definitely have found herself looking his way.

Instead, though, he was there standing on the Thorntons' doorstep, looking concerned and official. Paige also saw that he was looking straight past Prof. Thornton to her.

"Paige King?"

"Um... yes?"

Was she in some kind of trouble? Paige couldn't think of anything she'd done that might warrant the attentions of the FBI, but even so, she found herself worrying about it.

"My name is Agent Marriott. I'm with the FBI's Behavioral Analysis Unit. I need to talk to you urgently."

Paige felt the moments stretching out. A sudden sense of dread ran through her. Why would someone from the FBI take the trouble to find out that she was at her supervisor's house? What was going on?

"What's this about?" Paige asked.

"Adam Riker has escaped."

CHAPTER FOUR

For several seconds, Paige could only stare at the FBI agent in front of her in shock. She felt as if all the strength went out of her legs, so that she might stumble, and had to catch herself against the doorframe to stop it from happening.

"Escaped?" she managed. The full horror of what that might mean was still sinking in for Paige.

"Earlier tonight," Agent Marriott said. He looked to her, then to the Thorntons. "May I come in?"

Prof. Thornton looked over to her. "It's ok with us, Paige, but if you'd rather do this another time..."

He was obviously trying to protect her, but right then, Paige didn't need protection. She needed to know what was happening, and how Adam had managed to escape from a supposedly secure facility. More than that, she needed to know that everything possible was being done to put Adam back where he belonged.

"Maybe once I'm out, we'll talk again. On my terms."

The memory of those words made Paige feel almost sick with worry. At the time, the threat had seemed bad enough, but ultimately empty, since Adam wasn't going anywhere. After Dr. Neil had increased security, she'd almost been able to dismiss it completely, but now that he was out...

...now, it was terrifying. Now, it meant that Adam might be coming right for her.

"We're doing everything we can to catch him," Agent Marriott said. He'd obviously spotted the fear on Paige's face. "But the more we know about him, the easier that will be. That's why I was hoping to talk to you."

So this wasn't just a precautionary visit to warn her about the killer on the loose. No, of course not. FBI agents had better things to do at a time like this than just deliver warnings. He could have left that to the local police, or even just called. Agent Marriott thought that there was something to gain by talking to Paige. Maybe it would help to catch Adam quicker.

If it could, then Paige was more than willing to help. She wanted him back behind bars more than anyone.

"Yes, come in," Paige said. She looked over to Prof. Thornton. "If you're sure it's ok?"

"It's fine," Prof. Thornton assured her.

He showed them through to the lounge, rather than the kitchen. There, Paige quickly found herself ensconced on one end of an ancient leather sofa, with Agent Marriott on the other, Prof. Thornton on an armchair and Haley going to fetch coffee. Paige waited for Agent Marriott to make the first move.

"At the institute, they said that Adam Riker had told you that he was planning to escape," Agent Marriott said, in a neutral tone.

"That's right," Paige replied. "We had a counseling session earlier today."

Paige found herself thinking back through that session, wondering if there was anything more that she could have done to stop Adam from escaping. There was nothing, though. She'd done everything she could.

"And when he told you that he was going to escape, you told Dr. Neil, the institute's director?"

Paige nodded. "That's right. I hoped that he would take it seriously."

She saw Agent Marriott nod. "Very seriously. He doubled the guards on that wing. But then Riker used that confusion to make his escape easier."

Prof. Thornton stepped in then, obviously seeing where the FBI agent was going with that line of questioning. "You aren't suggesting that Paige played some part in Adam Riker's escape?"

Paige was touched by the note of protectiveness there, even as she was suddenly worried that the professor might have a point. What if this FBI agent thought that she'd helped Adam to escape? What if he was really here to accuse her of something.

Agent Marriott was already shaking his head, though. "No, I don't believe that you did that, Paige. I *do* believe that he manipulated you, though, to get you to give him what he wanted, even while you thought you were stopping him."

"So he played me?" Paige asked.

She didn't like the feeling of that, as true as it probably was. It was too close to the way Adam had revealed just how much he'd known about her. It was a reminder that their sessions hadn't just been her trying to learn all she could about the serial killer. It had been a battle for information that Paige hadn't even been fully aware she was fighting. And because she hadn't been aware of it, she'd been losing that battle.

"I think he has played a lot of people," Agent Marriott said, in a reassuring tone. "In one sense, you're the lucky one. He actually persuaded one of the guards to help him escape. That guard is now dead."

Paige winced at that, but she wasn't entirely surprised. "Adam doesn't see people as worth anything. They're just there to be controlled, and then discarded. He's good at making people believe that they're special, that they're the one who means something to him, and that's how he gets them to do what he wants."

She saw how pleased Agent Marriott looked as she said that. It seemed that Paige had done something right. It only took her another second to understand what.

"You're here because of my sessions with Adam," Paige guessed. "You think I have some kind of inside line on what he's going to do, and when."

"As I understand it, you've spent months having counseling sessions with him," Agent Marriott said. "That you're doing a big part of your doctoral thesis on him?"

Paige nodded. "That's right."

She could see where this was going.

"So you probably know Adam Riker about as well as anyone does right now. You're probably better placed to guess what he might do next than anyone else."

A few hours ago, and Paige might have agreed with him. She might have happily declared herself to be the world's biggest expert on Adam Riker. Now, though, after Adam had revealed just how much he'd learned about her in return, and after he'd used her to make his escape easier, she wasn't sure.

"I'll tell you anything I know," Paige said, hearing the uncertainty in her own voice. "But after all of this…"

Agent Marriott smiled her way. "Don't be too hard on yourself. Yes, he tricked you, but anyone can fall for a trick. You still know more than anyone else about all of this."

"He's right, Paige," Prof. Thornton said. "Remember, I've seen the drafts of your thesis. I don't believe that anyone could have fabricated the contents of those sessions for so long. You have a wealth of information on Adam Riker that no one else does."

It was good to hear her mentor's confidence like that, but Paige found herself just as comforted by Agent Marriott's words. This was a man who presumably faced up to the most dangerous of men every day, yet he was asking for *her* help.

"What do you need to know?" Paige asked, composing herself.

Agent Marriott leaned forward slightly. "Can you start by giving me a sense of what Adam Riker is like. I've seen the files on his crimes, but I want to know about the man."

Paige nodded. She could do that. Providing that kind of basic assessment was a part of what she'd done at the institute, after all.

"The first thing you have to understand is that he's highly intelligent," Paige said.

"But a psychopath."

Paige tried to work out the best way to explain it to the agent. "The two aren't mutually exclusive. If anything, the people we would call psychopaths are often highly intelligent. And… well, 'psychopath' is a difficult term."

"Because of the lack of an official diagnosis from the APA," Agent Marriott said.

Paige was impressed that he knew that, but then remembered that he was with the BAU. Of course, this would be exactly the kind of thing that he knew all about.

"That's right," Paige said. "But yes, on most common scales, Adam scores highly in terms of psychopathic traits. He has a lack of empathy, a lot of superficial charm, he's manipulative, tends to do extreme things to see what the reaction will be."

She saw Agent Marriott nod again. "All of that sounds pretty standard. But I'm not interested in standard. What is there about Adam Riker that makes him unique?"

That was the important part for something like this, Paige guessed. Agent Marriott would have hunted serial killers before, but this was about what made Adam Riker who he was.

Paige tried to think. She knew about Adam, but it was a question of trying to boil it all down to something coherent. It was the same thing she had to do with her thesis, but here, it mattered much, much more. She had to get this right.

"The big thing for Adam is control and manipulation," Paige said. "Even the way he kills his victims is about that. He restrains them in positions that lead to positional asphyxia, often after rendering them

30

unconscious, but other times after threatening them, or even tricking them into allowing it."

"Tricking them?"

That was one of the scariest parts of all of this. "There are at least a couple of cases where he set it up as some kind of sex game with his victim, and then killed them once they were helpless."

"So this is about sex for him?" Agent Marriott asked.

"No." That wasn't what Paige meant at all, and it was important that Agent Marriott understood the difference. "I'm pretty sure that sex doesn't matter much to Adam. It's all about power and control for him. He gets off just as much on manipulating someone into a trap where he can subdue them and restrain them. He literally strings his victims up like puppets."

"And then he tortures them," Agent Marriott said. He'd obviously read Adam's files.

"Sometimes," Paige explained. "We... I discussed this with him, and he listed the things he did to his victims so coldly and calmly. I didn't get any sense that he got any enjoyment out of that side of things directly. It was just another way for him to demonstrate how helpless they were and how much control he had. Sometimes, he said that he would just sit there and watch. I got the impression that he viewed the torture almost as a form of mercy, making them struggle and waste their strength more quickly."

Agent Marriott was silent for several seconds as he thought about that.

"If he's so deeply about control, there's a good chance that he might be hiding out with someone he has manipulated into helping him?" Agent Marriott asked.

Paige was impressed that he'd made that leap. "It sounds plausible."

"And there's a long history of people helping criminals, even though they know what they've done," Prof. Thornton put in.

Agent Marriott nodded again. "What else can you tell me about him?"

Paige tried to think of something else that might be useful. "He has to win with everything. Every conversation, every session. He has to have the last word. He has better impulse control than many psychopaths, making him capable of planning things over extended periods, but if he suffers a slight, or if it looks like someone is getting ahead of him in something, he has to get them back for it. He talked

31

about his father beating him as a kid, and how he waited years, knowing that he would kill him. He didn't lash out. He didn't kill him as soon as the opportunity arrived. He waited until he could do it the way he wanted to."

"He admitted to murder with you?" Agent Marriott said, sounding slightly surprised by that.

Paige shrugged. "He was already being held for multiple murders. I know some killers lie about what they have and haven't done, but he didn't seem to care about admitting to others. He hasn't tried to hide most of his killings. He could have made them look like home invasions or robberies. Instead, he leaves his victims displayed. I think that's another way of asserting control, by telling the police that they can't stop him."

"He's wrong about that," Agent Marriott said. He sounded confident, and Paige hoped that it was justified confidence. She hoped that he would be able to catch Adam quickly, put him back behind bars, and put an end to this. Not least because of the fear that Adam might be coming for *her*.

Paige found herself worrying that it wouldn't be that simple, though. She'd seen how manipulative and how clever Adam could be. She'd thought that she was giving away nothing in their sessions, but he'd known all about her life.

"Am I in danger?" she asked. "With the threats that he made?"

"I'm not going to let anything happen to you," Agent Marriott said, and there was something reassuring about the ease with which he said it. "We're going to catch him. Obviously, the more information you can give me on him for that, the better."

"I have recordings of my sessions with him," Paige said. "I guess I could send you my notes and transcripts for them."

"I'd like that," Agent Marriott said. He paused for a moment. "But what I'd like even more is for you to consult with me on this. Would you accompany me while I try to find him? I think your insight on the ground might be very helpful."

Paige saw Prof. Thornton bridle at that. "You're seriously asking Paige to put herself in harm's way, chasing after a serial killer?"

"She wouldn't be in harm's way," Agent Marriott promised. "I'd make sure of it. You wouldn't have to leave the car, Paige. You wouldn't have to go into any danger. I know you're a civilian. But I think your insights might be the best chance we have to actually catch this guy."

32

Paige shook her head, though, wanting to make it clear what she thought of the idea. Interviewing Adam in the controlled environment of a psychiatric institution was one thing but chasing after him was quite another. She wasn't about to do something as dangerous and impetuous as trying to hunt down a serial killer. She'd leave that to the professionals. To the people who actually had a chance of stopping him.

"I can't. I'm sorry, but I just… can't. But if you need anything, you can call me. Day or night."

She gave him her number. He was the kind of guy she might have given her number to anyway, but these were very different circumstances. She wasn't thinking about how good looking he was so much as how firmly she was going to lock her door when she got home, and how carefully she was going to check for intruders.

"And you're welcome to call me if you feel even slightly unsafe," Agent Marriott said, handing over his card. "Or if you remember anything that might help me find Riker faster. I also want to offer you protection. If Riker has threatened you, I can have the local police post people near you to watch in case he shows up."

Paige shook her head, though. She didn't want to take people away from the search. Besides, she wasn't sure it would do much good. If Adam truly wanted to get to her, Paige wasn't sure how much any of it would do to stop him.

In spite of Agent Marriott's reassurances, Paige didn't feel safe. She had a feeling that she wasn't going to get much sleep that night.

CHAPTER FIVE

Adam waited without moving in the bushes outside of the small, suburban house he was watching until he was sure that the whole neighborhood was safely asleep. He wanted to make sure that nothing would disturb him while he worked. He wanted to be certain that he would have all the time in the world.

He took the time to look over the house, taking in the cameras that dotted the outside, and the telltale flickering light of an alarm system. They were impressive security precautions for a simple house, a serious attempt to keep him out, but he had dealt with that kind of thing in the past. They wouldn't be enough to stop him.

He moved forward, hefting the bag he carried. He'd taken the time to change clothes and acquire supplies after breaking out, the means to do so already arranged as part of his plan. He had the resources he needed for this, and for everything else he needed to do. He was dressed in dark clothes, now, with black sneakers that would let him move silently, and a hooded sweater that hid his shape against the shadows of the neighborhood.

Adam crept close to the house, judging the line of his approach so that he was able to slide through the blind spots of the cameras as they swung back and forth to scan the perimeter. Would they be monitored at this time? He guessed that it was possible, but it didn't seem likely.

In any case, once he got to the power junction for the house, it ceased to be entirely relevant. Taking insulated pliers, he cut through the main cables, and saw the alarm system go dark. It wasn't the subtlest way to deal with things, but sometimes, the direct approach was the most effective.

That bought him a few seconds before the backups came on, and Adam was already running to the alarm box. He'd learned to disable alarms the same way that he'd learned other languages, or the best ways to render someone unconscious without killing them. He'd found it easy, when so many other people seemed to insist on how hard it was. They were all tools to let him do what he needed to without anyone trying to stop him.

The alarm's light flickered off, the system disabled for now. The locks were next on Adam's itinerary, and here was one part that the house's owner hadn't thought to upgrade. When Adam set to work with a couple of slender picks, the lock lasted barely a minute before it gave way to him, clicking open as easily as he might have forced open a padlock.

That was almost insulting. Just another reminder of how inferior the woman within was to him. How weak she was, compared to him.

He slipped inside, into a dark hallway with pictures set around it. Adam took a moment or two to look at those pictures by the light of a small flashlight, finding the ones that were of family of friends and taking them. It was one more small piece of this, one more thing to use in the moments that were to come.

With that done, Adam took more time to check the ground floor of the house, making sure that there were no unexpected surprises, that there was nothing there that might interrupt what was to come. It was better to be careful. He didn't want anything that might stop him. Not now.

He padded upstairs in near silence, every movement carefully judged, every step precise. He heard the creak of one of the stairs, and froze in place, listening for any reaction to the sound. Only when he was certain that there had been no response did he continue on upwards.

Adam didn't hesitate when he reached the landing. He knew which door he needed, knew the interior plan of the house perfectly. He moved over to it quickly. He set down his bag, and the pictures that he had taken from below, taking out a small bottle and a cloth. He let a few drops of the sedative seep into it, and then crept into the room.

The woman he had come to kill lay asleep on her side, a halo of hair curling around her face, one arm tucked under her head as if it made a better pillow than the one that she rested on. Her sheets were tangled, as if she'd kicked them about in the middle of a nightmare.

But then, she had every reason to have nightmares.

Adam padded closer, leaning over her, looking down, drinking her features in with his eyes, savoring this moment before he struck. In that moment, almost as if sensing his presence, her eyes snapped open.

Adam acted instantly, pushing the cloth with the sedative down over her mouth and nose. She fought, of course, because that was the kind of woman she was. She kicked out at both him and the covers frantically. Her hand flailed out towards a small side table, presumably where she now kept some kind of weapon. It was close by, but in this moment, it was out of reach. It might as well have been a thousand miles away.

There was nothing she could do to stop him now. Adam had made sure of it. It meant that slowly, under the influence of the sedative, her body seemed to accept it. She went limp, and Adam held the cloth there for another few seconds just to be sure that she wasn't feigning unconsciousness.

Then he went to his bag and got out his ropes.

He tilted the bed on its end to give him a frame to work with, and then started to lash his victim to it, arms up and wide, so that all her weight would hang from them. He gagged her with a bundle of cloth and some tape, then set about adding more layers of rope to contort her, turning her into exactly the kind of human puppet he wanted her to be. Once he was done with that, Adam started to set out the pictures he'd found downstairs around her. Just one more small torment, seeing all the people she would lose, all the fragments of her past that caused her pain.

Her eyes opened eventually, blinking awake slowly. She started to thrash in the bonds that held her, but Adam had tied them securely. He always did.

"Hello Eloise," he said. "It's good to see you again."

She tried to scream through the gag, but that didn't work. Adam was careful about these things. He wasn't about to allow anything that might stop this.

"You thought that you escaped me, last time," he said. "That you were so brave and determined that you managed to hold out until help came. Isn't that right, Eloise?"

She didn't give him a real answer, just kept straining at the ropes. Adam could see the stress already showing on her face as she struggled to pull herself upwards. He hoped that she wouldn't wear herself out *too* quickly. That would spoil the moment.

"The truth is that it was luck that saved you. Just luck, nothing else. If your boyfriend hadn't come around at *just* the wrong moment... well, you're going to see what would have happened."

Eloise's boyfriend had been meant to be away at a conference. Adam had checked. He'd been careful. Yet the boyfriend had come back early. Such a small thing to lose one's freedom over. Adam would make sure that things went differently tonight.

36

"I notice that you broke up with him," Adam said. "What was it? Were the nightmares too much for him? Did you scream every time he got close to you, after I'd visited you?"

She wasn't screaming now. Instead, she was quietly whimpering, fighting to raise herself up. She would be able to manage it for now. Not for long, though.

"I'm told that the position you're in has a similar effect to being crucified," Adam said. "Not that the religious symbolism matters to me, much. Other positions would work just as well. *Have* worked, just as well. But this... achieves a pleasing effect tonight. As you sink down, your shoulders will rise up, compressing your lungs. You will slowly suffocate."

He liked his victims to know what was going on before the end. It added nicely to their helplessness. It made them fight back, and those struggles only burned energy that they did not have. It was another pleasing way of reinforcing their position in this.

Adam moved close to her, watching the fear in her eyes. She was trying to plead with him now, as if that would achieve anything. As if it ever had, with any of his victims. She would plead, and bargain, and perhaps rage. Then, towards the end, there would be a beautiful kind of... acceptance. There would be just her and Adam there, in those last moments before her death.

There was nothing quite as beautiful as that. That moment... no one but Adam knew that moment. It was his, and his alone.

For now, though, there was the work. Adam took out a knife. It was short, and wickedly sharp. More than enough to make her move and rob her of her strength. He was in a mood to be generous about that. He held it up where Eloise could see it, letting the little light that filtered in through her bedroom window glint from the blade.

"Shall we begin?"

CHAPTER SIX

Paige saw Adam Riker stalking her a dozen different ways. He was following her down the street, just paces behind while a crowd of people ignored them both. He was there in her house, looming above her. He was standing in front of her, while Paige dangled in a web of ropes, unable to breathe...

Paige woke up gasping and clutching at her bedclothes, for what had to be the fifth time that night. Only it wasn't night anymore. Glimmers of golden sunlight were streaming in past the blinds over her apartment window, illuminating the room and making it impossible for her to shut her eyes again.

Paige checked the time: It was 8am, time to get up and get on with some writing on her thesis. It was definitely better than trying to sleep again when the darkness held only nightmares for her.

Paige got up and got dressed, in jeans and a deep blue sweater. She didn't have to go into work today, didn't have to rush to be at the institute on time for the first time in a long time. Her residency was finished, so all that was left was writing up her PhD.

All. That made it sound like some kind of easy thing, rather than a process of trying to draw together different strands that sometimes didn't want to go together. That would have been hard enough, even without Adam out there somewhere, on the run now.

One of the first things Paige did that morning was to walk around her apartment, checking that it was secure, because she wouldn't feel safe until she did so. It didn't take long. The kind of apartment a grad student could afford in Washington, D.C. was so small that a few steps could take her from one side of it to the other. The walls were a basic gray that Paige had tried to liven up here and there with pictures, mostly of far-off places she hadn't been yet, because there was never any time or money to do it. There was one of Mount Fuji, another of the Victoria Falls. Paige liked to stare at them while she worked on her thesis, reminding herself that being stuck in a room writing wasn't forever, that this wasn't the whole world, however much it might seem that way in academia.

Paige took the time to get coffee and then went to her laptop, knowing that she couldn't put the work off any longer and wanting to sift through the stacks of notes and files that she had. Most of her PhD thesis was written now, and had been through a dozen re-drafts, thanks to Prof. Thornton's input. Paige would come up with a draft of a chapter that she thought was close to perfect, would send it over to him, and would quickly find the return copy covered in comments asking questions she hadn't even considered.

Is Stern's theory of the self relevant here?

Expand with reference to the influence of neuro-psychology.

Would Hauser's approach to attachment theory explain this paragraph better?

Each one sent her off down a fresh rabbit-hole of investigation, with the result that this draft was something Paige couldn't even have contemplated writing when she began this process. Each run at it had felt as though it brought her closer to perfection.

More importantly, though, each one felt as though it brought Paige a little closer to actually understanding how serial killers like Adam Riker felt and thought. Each pass she took seemed to bring Paige a little closer to understanding whoever had taken her father from her. If she could just get deep enough into it, maybe it would all finally make sense.

Maybe she would be able to catch the man who'd done it and stop something like that from ever happening again.

Maybe there would finally be some kind of end to the memories that came to her unbidden, of staring down at her father's corpse.

That thought was normally enough to push Paige deep into her work, writing obsessively, when all the other doctoral students at Georgetown spent their time complaining about just how difficult they found that part of it. She loved getting lost in the words, trying to use them as a way into the ideas behind them. The words usually came almost as quick as her thoughts, so that the challenge was to slow down enough to make sure that what came out was good.

Today, though, Paige was having a harder time than usual. She couldn't focus, couldn't concentrate for more than a minute or two. The words wouldn't come, when normally they poured out in a flood. She sat there for at least ten minutes, just staring at the spot where she'd left off, reading and re-reading the last paragraph, hoping that it would spark something and set her writing again.

The problem was simple: Every time she tried to start, Paige found her thoughts drifting back to Adam, and those thoughts made it impossible to concentrate on the work.

It wasn't just the thought of him out there in the world, free to do whatever he wanted, although that was a part of it. It wasn't even the thought of the things he'd done to his victims, although the details of that had haunted Paige's dreams. She knew far too many of them, from her research. Adam had been only too willing to tell her everything, in that regard.

No, the part that kept coming into her mind, stopping her from thinking about anything else, was that last interview with him. Specifically, it was about that moment when he had announced that he was going to escape, obviously knowing exactly how Paige would react. The moment when he had revealed just how much he knew about Paige and about her family, showing just how efficiently he'd outwitted her in their sessions.

That was the hardest part of this, in some ways. Not the sudden danger, not the risk that a serial killer might be out there, coming for her. Not the possibility that he might be fixating on her, and she knew what happened to the people on whom he fixated. Just the fact that he'd already beaten her in one small way.

Paige found herself opening up her recordings of the sessions, trying to find the points at which she'd given away too much. Where had she gone wrong? Where had she let more slip than she should have done?

"Will you tell me something about yourself please, Paige?"

Paige heard Adam's voice on the recording and shivered. How many times had he asked that question? He'd made a game of it, asking again and again.

When Paige hadn't answered, she could remember the silences. It was as if he could feel how deeply Paige needed to get answers from him. He'd known that this wasn't just a piece of research for her. He'd known that he had a kind of power in withholding information.

"Paige King. That's a pretty name."

He'd said that, too, reading the name from one of her notepads. Paige should have taken that as her cue to run as far from Adam as she could, to find other patients to interview and leave him alone completely. It should have been a sign that he was trying to learn about her, and that he was far too dangerous to deal with. Paige should have walked away.

She hadn't, though. She hadn't thought that something as tiny as that would allow him to learn anything else about her. Prisoners weren't meant to have access to the outside world. Anyone outside could just have Googled her, but Paige had assumed that she was safe in an environment where Adam simply didn't have that kind of access.

Obviously, though, he did. Or he didn't need it. He knew all about her. He'd done his research.

He'd even traded information with her.

"If you want me to tell you about myself, then it's only fair that you tell me something in return."

Paige picked out that phrase from the recordings.

She'd done it, hadn't she? She'd reasoned that Adam wouldn't be able to do anything with the information he got from her. She'd thought that she'd limited what she told him. She'd thought that what she was getting in return was more than worth it.

She'd been very, very wrong.

Paige found herself wondering if she should call her mother. Should she warn her that there was a dangerous killer on the loose, and that he'd expressed far too unhealthy an interest in everything around Paige?

Something stopped Paige from picking up the phone to call. She told herself that it wasn't a good idea to panic her mother unnecessarily, but that wasn't the whole truth. The truth was that she didn't *want* to call her mom. Things were too complicated between them.

Besides, she knew Adam. If he was going to focus on anyone, then it was going to be her, slowly showing her how much better he was, before finally…

Paige had to drag her thoughts away from the prospect of everything that a killer like Adam might do to her. Those thoughts had occupied far too big a part of her nightmares already today. She had to remind herself that it was unlikely that he would come for her, and that even if he did, she was living in a secure apartment block, where people would see him coming.

Most likely, he would be caught before anything got that far. Paige had met Agent Marriott, and it was obvious that he knew what he was doing. Add to that all the state police and even marshals who would be hunting for Adam, and he would be lucky to stay out of custody for more than a day. Escaping wasn't the same thing as staying free.

Paige tried to tell herself that, but it was hard to really believe it when she'd spent so much time talking with Adam. She'd gotten him to do various puzzles, and even an IQ test, mostly by agreeing to do them alongside him, so that he could have the satisfaction of winning. It only occurred to her now that he'd been paying attention to her results just as much as she had to his.

He was highly intelligent, good at planning, and obviously motivated. If anyone could evade custody for an extended period, then it was him.

Paige tried to distract herself by scrolling the internet. She'd read somewhere that procrastination could be a useful part of the creative process. She went through her social media feeds, liking posts and trying to let her brain just switch off with a few undemanding memes. Maybe it would let her brain work out what she needed to do and get her into a space where she could actually write.

Then she saw the news story, sitting there on one of her friends' feeds like a toad squatting in a pond.

D.C. Woman Found Murdered. Is a serial killer to blame?

Paige tried to tell herself that it was probably clickbait, and that it didn't have to mean any of the things that she dreaded it might mean. She reminded herself of Betteridge's Law, that any title ending in a question mark could be answered with the word no. She couldn't stop herself from clicking, though, couldn't look away from the prospect that someone might already be dead at Adam's hands. She read on with growing horror.

D.C. police have today confirmed that local woman Eloise Harper was found dead in her apartment. While the police have declined to comment on her death, witnesses have suggested that she was found suspended and tortured in a manner consistent with the notorious serial killer Adam Riker, who yesterday escaped from a secure psychiatric institution. The police have so far declined to comment on the incident. More generally, they have stated that Adam Riker is an extremely dangerous individual and should not be approached. If you have any information on his whereabouts, call the number below.

Paige felt sick at the thought that Adam might have killed again, so soon after getting out. While the skeptical part of her didn't want to just trust some story that she'd found on the internet, there was one detail there that told her that the whole thing was far, far too real.

That name told her everything: Eloise Harper.

Paige knew that name almost as well as she knew her own. She'd heard it and read it, many times. Paige had never met her, but even so, she knew more about her than she did about most of the people she had met. Adam had told Paige about her in detail, dissected her life. He'd talked about her at length. About his feelings towards her, about her weaknesses and the ways he'd controlled her.

About the way he'd been caught trying to kill her.

That had been his regret: that he'd been caught, not anything to do with his actions. Not the fact that he'd been trying to kill someone in cold blood. He'd cursed his bad luck to Paige. He'd told her every detail of the things he'd been planning to do to Eloise. At the time, it had seemed like another of his little tests, trying to determine how strong Paige's stomach was. Trying to unnerve her because that would be another little win for him.

Now, Paige realized that he'd been telling her what he was planning to do. He'd been setting out, not what he wished he'd done, but what he was going to do next.

Paige knew that she couldn't just keep that information to herself. She snatched up her phone. She still had Agent Marriott's number and dialed it as quickly as her slightly shaking hands would let her. The phone rang for several seconds, and Paige found herself praying that it wouldn't go through to voicemail.

At last, Agent Marriott picked up the phone.

"Hi," Paige said. "It's Paige King, from last night."

"I remember," Agent Marriott said. He sounded pleased to hear from her. If things had been different, Paige might have been happy that he remembered her.

"I… I just heard the news, about the murder."

How was she meant to bring something like this up? It wasn't the kind of thing anyone had taught her, even working with killers as she did.

"If you're worried that this means Adam Riker is still close by, or about your safety, I can have the local police send a car around."

Paige realized that he thought she'd just been scared by the article. And she had, but it wasn't just that.

"No, I… this isn't about that," Paige said. "I recognized the name of his victim. Eloise Harper. That's the name of the woman Adam was trying to kill when he was caught. She was the one person who survived him. Who *beat* him."

"I know the name from the files," Agent Marriott said. "But you're saying that this is about him finishing what he started?"

Paige should have guessed that an FBI agent would also have made the connection. Even so, it didn't sound as if he understood all of it.

"More than that." Paige tried to find the right words, tried to think of a way to put it that might make some kind of sense. "Adam hates to lose at anything. He likes to prove his superiority. This was him finding a way to win."

There was a pause at the other end of the line as Agent Marriott thought about that. "Does he have any other unfinished business? Anywhere he might go next?"

"I don't know if he does." Paige looked across at her computer, with her copious notes on her sessions with him. If the answer was anywhere, it was in there. "But I could find out."

"And could you guess where he might go next, based on that?"

Paige should have expected that question. It was what everyone needed to know most, right then. They needed to work out where Adam was going to be, so that they might actually have a chance of catching him.

"Maybe," she said. She wanted to say that it was a nuanced business, and that even though psychology made claims of being a science, often its predictive power was anything but absolute. Somehow, though, she guessed that wasn't what Agent Marriott needed to hear right then.

On his side of the conversation, Agent Marriott didn't hesitate. "Then I need you here with me, Paige. Physically here, beside me, where you can see everything that's going on and tell me how it all fits into what you know about Riker. Your notes aren't enough. I need someone who can interpret it all in real time, on the ground. I know you're reluctant, but I'll do everything I can to keep you safe, and I really do think you're the best hope we have of finding him."

Paige hesitated. She'd wanted to keep out of the way of all of this last night, but her nightmares had already told her how impossible that was. Even if she did everything that she could to stay safe, that couldn't protect her against Adam. There was no defense she could put in place that he couldn't walk through easily. He'd told her in detail how he'd done it with his other victims.

Besides, she knew more than anyone about him. She had a chance to really help here, using her research to try to track him down before he could do any more damage.

44

Wasn't that what she'd wanted all along? To use her research to catch serial killers?

"All right," Paige said. "Just tell me where I need to go."

CHAPTER SEVEN

Paige sat in her tiny electric car with her laptop beside her, a little bit away from the crime scene Agent Marriott had invited her to, trying to resist the urge to just turn around and go home. She couldn't get mixed up in all of this. She *shouldn't* get mixed up in this. She was an academic. She couldn't go hunting for serial killers alongside the FBI.

Paige could feel the waves of fear underneath that, trying to hold her back. Adam was out there somewhere, and the last thing she should be doing was trying to get closer to him. She should be running, trying to put distance between the two of them. She should take a flight to Thailand, and sit on a beach, safe until all of this was done.

Paige fought back that feeling, because she knew from experience that running away from her fears didn't make things any better She forced herself to grab her laptop, step out of the car and survey the small suburban house in front of her. She wasn't going to be ruled by fear. Especially not when sitting at home wouldn't actually do anything to keep her safe. Not from Adam.

To Paige, the road around the crime scene looked completely crowded, even by the busy standards of D.C. She could see neighbors standing in their gardens, trying to get a view of what was going on. Reporters stood in crowds, held back only by the police tape and the presence of uniformed officers. She spotted TV vans parked wherever they would fit along the sidewalk, barely leaving enough room for her own small car.

The house itself would have seemed quite pretty to Paige if she hadn't known what had just happened there. It had white painted walls and a slate roof, with bushes ringing the edge of the garden, and a green painted front door. It looked like the kind of place someone might dream of to settle down in, rather than moving from rental apartment to rental apartment, the way she had since leaving Virginia.

Paige started forward towards the house, and she had to push her way through the crowd, because the reporters didn't seem to want to give way for anyone. They'd found their prime spots, and they weren't going to give them up for anyone. They were too intent on getting their scoop, their story. She would have thought that in D.C., even the most dramatic news story wouldn't have kept reporters standing there for long, because there was always another story clamoring for attention, in waves of politics and local events. The reporters here seemed determined, though.

Paige guessed that the story of Adam Riker escaping was too big for them to let go of, even with so many other alternatives available.

With an effort, Paige managed to find enough gaps in the crowd to push her way to the front, flowing through it like a fish cutting its way through a shoal until she pressed up against the police tape, where a large police officer blocked the way.

"Keep back from the tape please," he said, in a slightly bored tone that suggested he'd been saying it to people for most of the morning. Probably to reporters who hadn't bothered to listen to him.

"I'm meant to be here," Paige said, because she wasn't sure exactly what she was meant to say at a crime scene.

"Sure you are." There was no shift in the cop's tone. Obviously he'd heard this before. "What news site are you with, ma'am?"

Paige realized that she had no way of proving that she had been invited to be there, not without Agent Marriott's help. She got out her phone, ready to call him, and ask him to help her.

"She's with me."

Paige felt relief surge through her as she caught sight of Agent Marriott, striding out from the house and coming towards the line of police tape. She realized that for him to come out like this, he must have spotted her through the windows of the house. Perhaps he'd even been looking out for her. Paige kind of hoped that he had. She liked the idea of this tall, handsome FBI agent waiting just for her.

She pushed that thought away. It wasn't helpful. She was there to help catch a serial killer, after all.

She watched the police officer on duty lift the tape to let her pass, and just like that, she was able to step inside her first crime scene. Paige had seen plenty of pictures of such scenes, in books, and in the course of her work, but actually setting foot in a live scene was something else entirely.

Around her, camera flashes went off as the photographers reacted to the arrival of someone new at the scene. It didn't matter that the reporters probably didn't know who she was yet, just that she was there, being walked inside by an FBI agent. Would her picture be on the internet an hour from now, with a story talking about the expert consulting on the case? Would they take the time to work out who she was? Would they look into her past?

Paige didn't know whether to be proud of that or worried. What if they found out everything that had happened to her as a girl? What if *that* ended up on the news sites.

She had no doubt that if her picture was out there, Adam would see it. He would know that she was involved. She half suspected that he *wanted* her to be involved. He must have foreseen this possibility.

"I wasn't sure if you would come, even after you said you would," Agent Marriott said, as he started to lead the way back towards the house. Paige followed in his wake, stepping where he stepped, almost irrationally worried that to step anywhere else might lead to her stepping on evidence.

"I want to catch Adam as much as you do, Agent Marriott."

"Call me Christopher, if we're going to be working together," he replied with a smile that Paige had to admit lit up his features.

Paige tried to summon one in return, but the thought of what she was there to do made it hard. She couldn't smile at the thought of what might be inside the house.

"Nervous?" Christopher asked.

Paige nodded. "I've only seen pictures of crime scenes. I've never been into one."

"But you've looked at plenty of those for your research, I guess." He said it as if it were almost the same thing, rather than a world away.

"A few." Paige tried to explain it, and it was always hard, trying to sum up her research for someone who wasn't a specialist. "I'm mostly interested in the psychology of the killers, but sometimes that's reflected in the crime scenes they leave behind. The way they do things can tell us about the way they think, and so what they might do next."

"I hope that's the case here," Christopher said. He kept leading Paige towards the house, past the police controlling the scene. "As far as my superiors are concerned, you're a consultant. You shouldn't have any trouble from any of the cops around the crime scene, but if you do, send them my way."

She saw a couple of forensic specialists working around the edges of the house, conducting what looked like a fingertip search of the exterior. Paige saw one of them put a couple of tiny fragments into plastic bags, the sheer painstaking care of it impressive. She thought that she was thorough in her interviews with the prisoners back at the

48

institute, but even she could never imagine searching an area quite so carefully.

"Is it possible to tell anything about someone from their home?" Christopher asked, as they approached the house.

Paige guessed that, since he was with the BAU, he already knew the answer to that. It was just a question to get her thinking about the crime scene, rather than about the enormity of everything that was happening. Paige appreciated the effort on his part to make her feel like she belonged there.

Paige tried to look at the house again. "Maybe. People sometimes choose houses just because it's what they can afford at the time, but the general type of place they choose reflects something about their priorities at the time. This place seems like Eloise Harper was looking for something simple and normal."

Then she spotted the cameras, dotted around the edge of it, pointing out at the world and watching it carefully for any sense of danger.

"But it wasn't normal for her," Paige said, as she realized the implications of them. "All those cameras. She was living her life in fear. She was afraid that Adam would come back for her."

She'd had a small taste of what it was like to live with that kind of fear, both when she was younger, and last night, worrying about what would happen if Adam came for her. She could imagine only too well what it must have been like for Eloise.

"And he did," Christopher said, the happiness that had been there when he'd first seen her vanishing behind a mask of serious professionalism. "Are you ready to go inside, now? You don't have to if you don't want to. I could bring you photographs, or even just describe the scene."

"You don't need to do that," Paige said, even though she wasn't sure that it was true. She wasn't sure that she would ever be quite ready. She knew, though, that she would have the best chance of helping if she saw this for herself.

She followed Christopher towards the front door of the house, taking a breath as she stepped inside.

The smell of death hit her, and Paige knew that smell all too well. In an instant, she was back standing over her father's body, staring down at it in the kind of horror that had made her run as a small child. Paige had to hold herself in place then. She wasn't a girl anymore. She understood what was going on, and she wasn't about to give into the fear.

"Are you all right, Paige?" Christopher asked.

"I'm fine," Paige lied, and forced herself to move through the house after him.

The house was probably busier than it had ever been, with police and forensics officers seeming to fill every corner of it as they worked. Paige wasn't sure what they were looking for, when they already *knew* who had committed this crime.

Even so, it felt strangely empty and quiet. Maybe that was just because Paige knew what had happened there, or maybe it was because she knew what the normal sounds of a home were.

The result was a sense of wrongness that seemed to fill the house the same way the scent of death did. That scent hung in the air, impossible to mistake for anything else. It lingered in Paige's nose, and some part of her knew that it would still be with her even once she was well clear of the house. It would stay in her memories, and probably invade her dreams.

Paige tried to focus on the contents of the house, tried to do what Christopher wanted her to and learn something about Eloise Harper from its contents. That meant that she spotted something else was wrong almost instantly as she made her way through the house: a series of picture hooks that didn't have anything on them, most of them with faint shadows of fading around them to show that there definitely had been something there, rather than hooks waiting to be filled.

"Where are all the pictures?" she asked as Christopher led her upstairs.

"You spotted that?" the agent sounded slightly impressed. "They're... well, you should see it for yourself."

They reached a bedroom, where there were a couple more forensics people working, looking almost alien in their plastic evidence suits. Paige saw a bed tilted on its side, the cut remains of ropes hanging from it. Around the bed were pictures set out as if the whole thing were some kind of shrine. Paige could see blood stains on the floor.

"I need the room," Christopher said, with a note of authority, and the forensics people hurried to get out of the room.

That left Paige in there with him, and Christopher looking at her expectantly.

"Is it all right for us to be in here?" Paige asked. "I'm not disturbing evidence, or anything?"

"We know who did this," Christopher replied. "What matters now is catching him. Tell me what you see, Paige."

Paige felt as if this were some kind of audition, but she already knew what she was looking at. She was standing in the spot where a woman was killed, looking at the aftermath of that death. This felt a lot more involved than sitting opposite a serial killer, talking to him, had been. That felt almost safe by comparison.

"This is Adam," Paige said. "He strung her up, and he tortured her. My guess is the pictures were a part of that. He would have told her all about the people she would never see again. He… he likes to get a reaction out of people. He likes to try to show them that he can control everything they do. He wants to torment them psychologically as well as physically."

She saw Christopher nod. "That's consistent with what you told me back at your supervisor's house, but I need more than that. We know who this is, Paige."

Paige nodded. This wasn't about proving Adam's guilt, but about catching him. She needed to give Christopher something more than that, something that might actually help him to get closer to Adam.

Paige tried to think. Maybe if she could help him work out Adam's motivations, it might help?

"I think this is about Adam tying up loose ends," Paige said. "This was the one person he tried to kill that he failed to kill."

"But now he has," Christopher pointed out. "Does he have any *other* loose ends?"

"I'd have to go back through my notes to try to find them," Paige said. "We had a lot of sessions. I transcribed them for my thesis. I might be able to find something in there."

Christopher looked suddenly intent. "Then start looking. If it can give us anything that we need, then it will be worth it."

"*What* do you need?" Paige asked. It seemed better than trying to guess at things until she hit on what the FBI agent needed to hear. "The more of an idea you can give me of what you want, the better."

She saw Christopher pause to think for a moment or two. "The goal right now is to work out where he might go to next. Understanding him better will help with that, but right now, it's about finding places that he might go. Possible targets, possible places he might want to lay low, anything like that."

Paige could do that, or at least, she hoped that she could. It felt strange opening up her laptop in the middle of a crime scene to get at her files, but she did it, tapping away at it as she tried to isolate the right parts of her notes.

51

The problem was that there were so many of them. She'd had months and months of sessions with Adam, and after the first couple, he'd talked a lot. Paige found herself wondering if she could use word searches through her notes or through the transcripts of the sessions to find what she was looking for; yet even for that, she would need to have an idea of what she was trying to find.

Paige wracked her memory, trying to think of what she needed. She put her fingers to her temples as she tried to concentrate. A flash of memory came to her, and she started to work through her notes, searching for the one section of them that she needed.

"You've thought of something, haven't you?" Christopher said. He sounded suddenly hopeful.

Paige nodded. "Adam talked about a place in his sessions where he used to stay. A place that not even the police knew about. He boasted about how carefully he'd hidden it, putting the property in a false name. For a long time, he wouldn't tell me that name. He made me work for it. I had to pretend that I didn't believe him, but eventually, he just had to show off how clever he'd been. He told me, so that I could look it up and see just how expertly he'd arranged things."

"So you looked it up?" Christopher said. "You have an address for a possible safe house for this killer?"

Paige nodded. She did, and if they were lucky, her notes might mean that they were able to catch Adam Riker before he was able to kill again.

"All right," Christopher said. "Give me the address. You can wait here and-"

"I want to come with you," Paige said. The words were out of her mouth before she could stop herself. "I need to be a part of this. After all...," she gestured to the crime scene. "I need to be there for it."

Christopher looked as if he was going to argue, but he nodded, instead. "All right. But if we're going, we have to go *now*."

CHAPTER EIGHT

Paige rode out in Agent Marriott's car towards the address that she'd found for Adam Riker's safe house, wondering all the time if he would be there, if she would actually have found the escaped serial killer.

Wondering at the same time if she should be there, when being there potentially put her in danger.

It was obvious that Christopher could see how nervous she was as they left D.C., heading out into the countryside beyond.

"You're doing great, Paige," he said. "You handled the crime scene well, and without you, we wouldn't have a clue where to go to find Riker."

Paige appreciated the praise, but it didn't do anything to change the fact that soon, she might be coming face to face with a serial killer. One whose danger she understood probably better than anyone.

"Why don't you tell me about yourself?" Christopher suggested, and now it was clear that he was trying to take her mind off things. "Why are you working at a psychiatric institution?"

"I guess…I wanted to help people," Paige admitted. "I was feeling pretty... lost."

She didn't mention the death of her father, or the fact that she'd been the one to find him. She didn't mention her mother's new husband, or everything that had happened afterwards. Paige had gotten good at not mentioning those parts of herself. She'd worked out a long time ago that people either didn't want to hear those parts, or they wanted to hear about them far too much.

"I didn't know what to do with my life, and I found that working with people who had made terrible mistakes, I might be able to do some good. I wanted to understand them. I thought that if I did, then I might be able to help them."

"I can see the appeal," Christopher replied. "I don't know if I'm helping anyone with my job, but I guess it makes me feel better to know that I'm waiting for the bad guys. I'm going to be a little happier when we catch this guy, though."

"I know you will," Paige replied. She still couldn't think of herself actually catching Adam. She'd leave that part of things to the professionals.

"So where are you from?" Christopher asked. "I don't think I've heard it mentioned yet."

"I'm from Virginia," Paige replied. "A small town. You wouldn't have heard of it." Or if he had, it would be in the context of her father's murder, and that would tell him more about her than she was comfortable giving away, just then. "What about you? Why did you get into law enforcement? What made you join the FBI and the BAU?"

She wanted to keep the conversation going. She liked Christopher, but it was much easier to talk about him than about her past.

"I guess I just wanted to help people," Christopher replied. "I thought working in law enforcement would be the best way to do that. I wasn't interested in being a lawyer, and I thought the FBI would be an interesting challenge."

"And the BAU?" Paige asked.

"I like understanding people, and I'm good at drawing people out, at getting them to talk about what really happened. These are the kinds of cases that I like."

Paige couldn't help thinking that this was true of her job, too. It wasn't exactly the same, but she liked dealing with people who were thought of as the worst of the worst, trying to get some kind of truth out of them, understanding why they did what they did. She liked getting answers where other people believed that there weren't any to be found.

Christopher kept going. "A part of me wishes I could be a profiler, but all I'd do is ride shotgun in the car. I guess I got put on this team because I read a lot of books, and I know a little about most things. I'm a bit of a nerd when you get right down to it."

"I'd hardly say you were a nerd," Paige replied. He certainly didn't look like one. He looked more like an all-action kind of guy. The kind the BAU might send out once all the experts there had worked out exactly where to send him.

Paige was so caught up in the conversation that she didn't realize they'd arrived at the safe house until Christopher parked the car, pulling up a little way from the house in a sheltered spot. She looked up, suddenly realizing that although she knew about this place and had looked it up online, that was very different to seeing it close up.

They were outside of D.C. now, out in the country. Adam might hunt in and around the city, but his life was mostly beyond it.

The safehouse was an old farmhouse, so rickety looking that it seemed to Paige as if it might blow down the next time a storm hit it. There were a few outbuildings, including a large barn, wooden doors shut firmly against the world. They looked just as badly maintained, one smaller shed leaning over as if it were just on the verge of collapse.

Looking around, Paige saw a collection of old machine parts scattered across the yard, and empty fields beyond, leading to a small stretch of woodland, with no sign of civilization for miles. She found herself thinking that it was the kind of place where Riker could do what he wanted to someone, and no one would ever hear.

Had he ever killed anyone here? Mostly he killed his victims in their homes or offices, but that was only as far as anyone knew. He could have killed more people here without anyone knowing.

That thought brought a thrill of fear. What if he was here, watching them now? They were trying to catch him, but what would happen if they actually caught up with him? There was no denying just how dangerous Adam was, and out here, she and Christopher didn't have any back up.

Christopher got out of the car. "Stay here," he told her.

Paige shook her head, though. "I'm pretty sure the safest spot is right beside you."

She definitely didn't want to sit quietly in the car, waiting for the possibility that Adam might sneak out while Christopher was inside.

As such, Paige followed Christopher towards the house, keeping low and trying to stay out of sight, feeling nervous. Something felt off about this whole place. That was just what was going through Paige's head, but maybe it was more than that.

"Does this feel as creepy to you as it does to me?" Paige asked, and then realized that she should be trying to look more professional in front of the FBI agent. She was meant to be there as a consultant, not as some worried tag along.

"It's a bit run down," Christopher replied, "but I'm sure it's just fine."

They paused at the front door. It hung open and unlocked.

He led the way through the rickety old door, into what looked like a living room. Paige couldn't imagine anyone living here, couldn't imagine Adam staying here, but he'd told her that he had. She wondered if Riker was the only one who'd stayed here, or whether he had other accomplices. He was good at manipulating people to help him.

"Hello?" Christopher called out, his voice echoing through the empty house as he gave up on trying to move quietly. "Is there anyone there? This is the FBI!"

The large empty rooms of the house threatened to swallow up his voice, echoes seeming to come from its nooks and crannies. Obviously, the idea was to get some kind of reaction out of Adam if he was there.

"Hello?" Paige called out, adding her own voice to it. She half-suspected that if Adam was there, he might answer when he heard her voice, just for the effect that he could have on her.

If there was anyone there, though, they didn't answer. If Adam was waiting there, it was silent and in the shadows.

Both she and Christopher were looking over their shoulders as they walked, to make sure they weren't ambushed by Riker. Paige couldn't help feeling that they were making a mistake, moving through the place, that they weren't safe here.

"Riker, if you're there, give yourself up," Christopher called out.

It was as if the silence in the house was fighting to keep hold of them, to keep them from stumbling into the rooms that Adam Riker had been in. Paige shivered, looking around nervously and trying to make some sense of the emptiness of the place.

Something about the house was beginning to unsettle Paige more than she wanted. She wanted to get out of it, but at the same time, she wanted to know more about the man who had killed so many, wanted to know about the man who had escaped from prison and who might be here now.

Paige was looking around the front room, trying to spot anything that would tell her more about Adam Riker.

There was some old furniture, covered in dust. There were pieces covered in sheets, as if someone had been waiting to decorate the place, or as if they'd just closed off the whole building, waiting for its owner to return. There were absolutely zero personal items there, as if the idea of having anything warm or homey there were anathema to the owner, or as if he were being deliberately careful about leaving any trace of himself.

That made Paige feel hopeful. It felt exactly like the kind of thing Adam would do, trying to leave no trace, trying to make it as hard as possible for anyone to find anything real about him.

They made their way through the house carefully, checking every room. Christopher had a blocky pistol out ready, obviously in case Adam chose to attack them, but he didn't need it. They cleared the last room. There was no sign of Adam Riker.

"It's like he's a ghost," Christopher said.

Paige didn't reply to that, instead just looking at the old rooms with their hand-made furniture, their blankets and quilts. She tried to imagine the family that had lived here a hundred years ago, people who probably weren't really related to Adam Riker. This was just a place that he'd bought as a bolt hole.

"I guess he's not here," Christopher said, sounding disappointed.

Paige wasn't convinced yet. There were so many rooms, and Riker could have hidden almost anywhere. It was entirely possible that he was there, and that he was just waiting for the right moment to make his move.

"I just don't think we've looked in the right place," Paige replied, thinking of the old barn. "There are still the outbuildings."

The barn was the one building on the property that was closed up. Paige swallowed, suddenly realizing that this was the perfect place for a killer like Adam to hide. Better than the main building, in a lot of ways, because he would assume that anyone arriving to search would go there first. He could be watching them right now, waiting until they were close enough to attack.

Or he might have slipped away, already.

"We'll check the outbuildings," Christopher said. He led the way back out of the house, moving towards the barn. The two of them went quickly, not wanting to spend more time out in the open than they had to. They picked their way between the discarded machinery, and Paige was only too aware that they would make great targets if someone were watching them with a weapon.

They reached the barn and Christopher opened the door, taking a breath and going inside. Paige followed him, looking around nervously.

The barn was mostly empty. There were a few pieces of old machinery, a couple of old cars, and a few stacks of furniture. Paige could see that it used to be quite a large building, but now it seemed to be falling apart.

As with the house, there was no sign of Adam Riker.

Paige could see an old tractor sitting nearby, and a whole bunch of old furniture and equipment, but there was no sign of Riker, and no sign that anyone had been there recently.

Paige felt dejected in that moment. She'd been so sure that this would be the place where they would find Adam, where they would be able to end all of this, but instead, they'd found empty buildings. She'd led Christopher on a wild goose chase.

That was when Paige heard the sound of footsteps outside.

For a moment or two, Paige could barely breathe. Had they found him, just when it seemed that they'd come to an empty place?

She looked out, and there, by the side of the house, was a figure, bundled up in a jacket and hooded sweater. He took one look at her and Christopher there and turned to run.

CHAPTER NINE

Paige was sure in that moment that it was Adam. Who else could it be, and why would they run? Here, now, in the bolt hole that Adam had boasted about? It had to be him.

She looked at Christopher, who gave a nod, and set off at a run after the fleeing figure.

"Stay here!" he called back.

Paige hesitated only a moment or two before she ignored that and went with him, trying to avoid the chaotic sprawl of machinery in the farmyard. As the figure sprinted from the yard into the fields beyond, Paige did her best to keep up with Christopher.

They ran after the man in the hooded top, all thoughts of safety gone from their minds. Paige was aware that they were running across an open field, and that they would make perfect targets if it turned out that Riker had a weapon, but she put that out of her mind. They were catching Riker, and she wasn't going to let him get away now.

"FBI, stop!" Christopher yelled, running hard. The figure ahead showed no signs of slowing in response to his demand.

They were running through a field of wheat now, the figure in front of them zigging and zagging as if he expected Christopher to start shooting at any moment. He didn't slow down, though, and the wheat made it hard going, so that Paige had to push her way through it almost as if she were swimming.

She could see the figure running ahead of them still, pushing his own way through the wheat, dodging and weaving as if he knew exactly what he was doing. He was heading for a fence, with a stretch of woodland beyond it, and Paige realized that if he reached it, then it would be easy for him to climb over it and lose them in the trees.

"He's getting away!" she yelled to Christopher.

He glanced over, and then looked at her, and then back at the figure. He had his gun raised but shook his head even as Paige watched. "I haven't got a clear shot."

The figure was still running. He was clearly desperate to get away, but he was struggling to do it against the strong resistance of the wheat.

"FBI, stop!" Christopher called out again, as if it might do something. Maybe he was hoping that if he distracted Adam enough while he ran, there might be a chance of him tripping, allowing them to catch up.

The figure was getting farther ahead, and Paige was beginning to realize that they were never going to catch him while they were in the field.

They were so close to Adam, but now it looked as though he might get away in spite of that.

Paige ran as fast as she had ever run in her life, her feet sinking into the soil, her lungs burning. She couldn't let Adam get away, but he was ahead of them, and they weren't gaining on him.

Then, suddenly, he was through the field and making for the woods. Paige felt almost sure that would be the end of their hunt, because once he was in the trees, they wouldn't be able to keep a line of sight to him. Adam could slip away in any one of a dozen directions.

He disappeared into the trees, but Paige wasn't about to give up. She and Christopher leapt over the fence, following their quarry into the small patch of woodland.

There was no sign of him now, though. He'd already used the cover of the trees to break contact with them.

Paige found herself running forward blindly for several seconds, not knowing where she was going. She brought herself to a halt and looked around, looking for any sign of Adam, while Christopher scanned the area carefully with his gun out.

"Can you see him?" Christopher asked. He sounded slightly out of breath after so much running, but it was nothing compared to how exhausted Paige felt.

Paige shook her head. She didn't have the breath for more than that right then. She was certain that he was here somewhere, but there was no trace of him now. "No."

"Did he go left or right?"

Paige looked around. She was half-convinced that he'd darted left as he entered the woods, but she wasn't sure now. She didn't want Riker to get away, to vanish again, so she decided to make a choice. "Left."

Christopher nodded at that. Paige just hoped that she'd done the right thing, choosing the direction that she felt was right. They set off, crashing through the trees, but the figure had gone.

"Shit," Christopher said. "He must have doubled back."

Paige stared at her feet, feeling foolish. She'd been so sure she was right, so sure that she knew where he would be, and yet she'd been completely wrong.

"Come on," Christopher said, grabbing her arm. "He can't have gone far."

Paige followed her partner's lead, feeling foolish. They made their way back.

"We can't give up," she said, but she heard the uncertainty in her own voice, and knew that Christopher would be able to hear it too.

"He might have come back this way," Christopher said.

They made their way back through the woods, picking their way carefully through the thicket. Paige still had the feeling that Riker was out there, but where?

She started looking around, determined to find some sign of him. She tried to think. Where would he have gone? Would he be trying to put distance between himself and them?

One thing occurred to her: there were no sounds of someone running. She and Christopher had made plenty of noise passing through the woodland in their pursuit of Adam, but now everything was still.

That meant that he couldn't still be fleeing. Instead, Paige guessed that he would be hiding somewhere, probably watching. He would know that running now would draw too much attention, and only serve to give away his position. He would pick a hiding spot and wait, then try to double back and get clear once he was sure that he wouldn't be spotted.

"I think he's hiding somewhere," Paige said.

Christopher nodded. "You check over there. Stay in sight and call out immediately if you see anything."

Paige didn't like the idea of splitting up like that, but she knew that it was their best chance of actually finding Adam, so she moved off, looking around as she went. She glanced back, saw Christopher moving through the trees and she turned back to her task.

He had to be in the area, she knew. He had to be, but where was he? She walked around, trying to find a spot where he might be hiding. She glanced around, and then she saw it.

"Christopher!" she called.

He came running over, and she pointed to the figure, sitting in the shadow of a tree, in a hollow that hid him from sight from every other angle.

"Come out with your hands where I can see them!" Christopher called out, his gun out and aimed.

The figure got to his feet and started to run again.

Christopher fired off a warning shot, which struck a nearby tree, sending fragments of wood flying in every direction. It didn't slow their suspect down at all. If anything, it spurred him on to greater efforts, weaving in and out of the trees.

They were gaining ground on him now, though. Christopher was pulling ahead of Paige, closing the gap between him and the suspect.

He got close enough to tackle him, and he dived, throwing the man to the ground.

The moment Christopher had tackled him to the ground, the man let out a high-pitched cry. The two men fell, Christopher on top of their suspect Paige heard the sound of scuffling, and saw the man trying to fight back, but Christopher was on top, trapping his arms and wrenching one of them to force him to turn over to his stomach.

"Shit!" Paige heard the man yell. "Ouch! That hurt! You can't do this!"

"You can't run from us!" Christopher called. "You're under arrest!"

Even as he did so, though, Paige was realizing something that made her heart sink:

This wasn't Adam Riker. It wasn't his voice, and as he tried to fight back, it had none of the violence that Paige knew Adam was capable of. That would have been a hard fight for Christopher, against a man prepared to do anything to maintain his freedom. Instead, he was handling this man easily, pinning him in place and handcuffing him.

"It's not him, Christopher," Paige said, not able to contain the disappointment in her voice. She felt empty in that moment. She'd found a clue that she'd hoped would lead to Adam, but instead, it had led to someone else.

Christopher hauled the man up to his feet, pulling his hood from his head, to reveal a bearded, dirt-streaked face surrounded by lank hair. Paige could see the fear in the man's eyes.

It wasn't Adam. This man didn't look anything like him.

"Who are you?" she asked. Paige needed to understand why this man was here, in the spot where she'd been so sure she would find Adam.

"I'm no one," he said.

Christopher shook him slightly. "What's your name?"

"I'm Bert. I'm nobody. I didn't mean any trouble."

"What are you doing here, Bert?" Paige asked.

"It was empty! No one was using it, and I wanted to get out of the rain for a while. Then I stayed, because... well, why not? If there's been a complaint, I'll go. I don't want any trouble."

Did he really think that this was about trespassing? That the FBI got called in for that kind of thing? Paige guessed that he was too scared, or too troubled, to think about that clearly right then. But then, what else was he meant to think? It wasn't as if he knew about the manhunt that had brought Paige and Christopher there.

"Has anyone else been here?" Christopher asked. He obviously still wasn't giving up on the possibility that Riker had used this place as a bolt hole. "Someone who would have come in last night or earlier today?"

The homeless guy shook his head, though. "No, there's been no one but me."

"You're sure?"

Paige saw him nod. "I'd tell you if there had been. I don't want any trouble."

Which meant that they'd come to the wrong place. Paige had *led* them to the wrong place. She'd been so sure that she'd found where Adam would try to hide, but instead, she'd just wasted time that they could be using to try to catch up to him.

Paige realized something worse in that moment: Adam had tricked her.

When he'd mentioned the house in his sessions, he must have known that Paige would look into it. He'd planted the seed of this place, precisely because he'd known that when he escaped, someone would ask Paige for her opinion about where he might go. Of course, he wouldn't come here after that. He'd sent them in the wrong direction, and bought himself time to either escape...

...or to do something else. Something worse.

CHAPTER TEN

Adam guessed that another man in his position might have spent his time hiding from the authorities. A man who had just broken out of a secure psychiatric institution ought to be hiding, ought to be running, trying to get to a border. He'd heard about plans like that from the men in there: that if they could just get to a country with no extradition treaty, they could live out their lives untouched by the police, or even continue with their various little... interests.

Adam thought that they all thought too small. That they misunderstood what life would be like, if they ever succeeded in leaving.

No, there were some things that could not be avoided. It was hard to stay free forever. That was why it was vital to make the most of the time that one did have on the outside.

Because of that, Adam wasn't hiding. Instead, he was currently stalking Sara Langdon, keeping well back from her in the streets of Washington D.C., making sure that she didn't catch sight of him. Adam kept his face hidden under a hooded shirt and behind dark glasses, but even so, he was sure that she would recognize him if he got too close. She knew him far too well to be fooled by a disguise.

She looked very different from how he remembered her, tall and elegant, dressed in a dark skirt, blouse and jacket. Her hair was long and black and her eyes looking big behind the glasses she wore. She was just as perfect as always, but now she looked carefully put together, utterly in control of everything around her, rather than wild and chaotic.

Adam had to hang back, not being able to follow her as closely as he would like because of the risk of being spotted. It was easier when he was just another face in the crowd, but today, there weren't enough people on the streets for that to work. He knew where she was going, though. She was going to her office, a small place just up from Constitution Avenue that she used for her work. It was her pride and joy, and he could tell that she loved it.

The way she'd once pretended to love him.

He could approach her now. Could just walk up and do what he intended in the street. That would be too quick, though. Too easy.

She had been like that ever since she was a teenager. She'd been one of the strongest girls in their school, but she'd never taken a backward step from anyone, never backed down from a fight. He'd once seen her threaten to stab a bully. That was why he'd liked her so much.

She'd made his life more complicated, but he had never regretted it at the time. It had felt as though she was the first person that Adam could truly be himself around. He'd hurt her, of course, but never too much. She'd even pretended to enjoy it. She'd been there with him to commit small crimes, the kind of things that could only draw a couple like them closer together.

He'd never wanted to kill her.

Until she disappeared from his life without a backward glance.

Even then, he'd let her live. She was too special to kill. There was too much of a connection between them. He'd killed others in her place to assuage the feelings, just as he'd killed to deal with everything in his past. But he'd let her live, watching from a distance.

She'd been his everything. She'd been the one he had a special connection with.

Now, she wasn't, and Sara Langdon was going to die.

Not here, though.

He had no doubt that if he tried to approach her now, she would be ready for him. She'd probably have a pocket full of pepper spray and a knife hidden somewhere under that suit, even if this was some new, neater version of her. She'd have her keys between her fingers. She would be ready to fight, the way she always had been.

This wasn't the place, so he kept following her from a distance, making sure that she didn't see him.

Sara was getting close to her office building now. Adam watched her go inside, and then he waited for a minute, letting himself get as close as he could to the building. He checked for cameras before he moved, though, making certain that his face wouldn't be spotted.

He didn't want to be caught, after all.

He moved when he was sure there were no cameras looking his way. The door to the office building was locked, and there was an intercom system. He would be able to get around that when the time came. Adam knew the layout of the building that Sara worked out of. He'd scoped it out a few weeks before, using the internet access he wasn't meant to have back at the institution. He'd plotted out his way in, but wanted to check things on the ground.

Adam had learned the hard way to be careful about these things.

So he sat opposite the building, watching people come and go. It was an office building, with plenty of people moving in and out. It was obviously too busy right now, but later in the evening, it would be quiet. Sara had always been a night owl, and Adam was willing to bet that she worked late now. Then he could take his time with her.

So he waited, sitting on a bench on the opposite side of the street. Going into a bookstore so that he could buy a book to pretend to read as the day wore on, so that no one would grow too suspicious about him just sitting there. He caught sight of a few people heading for the entrance, and the building's ground floor restaurant.

He sat there, making notes about who was coming in and when. He had to get this right. Sara was dangerous. She knew him. She would be watching for him.

While he waited, he pulled out a bottle of water from his bag, took a swig, and looked at his watch. He had plenty of time. If he'd judged her right, Sara was likely to be in the office late into the evening, long after everyone else there had left.

That would be the moment that he struck.

While he waited, Adam found himself thinking about Paige King, the psychologist who had spent so much time talking to him back in the institution and trying to understand him.

She really thought that she'd found out the truth of him, asking him questions day after day. She'd gotten a whole thesis out of it, after all. An impressive amount to write, based on what he'd told her.

She really did think that she had him all figured out, but she was wrong. Her criminal profiler's mindset had blindsided her. She'd looked at a few bodies and thought that she knew how the killer behind them worked. She wanted to profile Adam. She wanted to find out who he was and why he did the things that he did.

He could laugh about it, really. She was right about some of it, but not nearly enough. She hadn't gotten to the truth. Not yet. It had been fun to let her think that she knew things about him. He'd even encouraged her, using their sessions to confide in her, to open up to her. She'd never guessed all the ways in which he was just lying to her.

Oh, not constantly. There were some truths in there, of course. It was important to season the lies with enough truth to make the whole believable.

Besides, he hadn't wanted *everything* he told her to be a lie, not when he'd started to see the connection between them.

He'd always known that she was smart. The fact was, though, that she hadn't known him as well as he'd known her. She had thought that she'd understood him, but Paige King had never really understood him. He'd been the one learning about her. He'd learned about her family, about her father's death, and about all the things that her new stepfather had done to her.

Paige had been the one asking the questions, but Adam had been the one getting answers. He knew her better now than she knew herself.

He'd been quite surprised to find that he liked what he'd found. There was something about Paige's gentleness, a kind of empathy that he couldn't really get enough of even as he despised the lie of empathy in everyone else. He'd loved being able to make her react, to see her squirm, to even hear her laugh during their sessions. The truth was, he'd liked her from the start, but it had taken him a while to admit it to himself.

It had taken time to see past it all, to understand the heart of her.

He'd been sure, briefly, that he'd never be able to hurt her. Then he'd been sure that he was going to kill her slowly, seeing exactly how long it would take for her to break before she died.

Now, things felt far more... ambivalent. Paige felt special. Adam wanted to be close to her and to hurt her, all at once. He'd learned about her to make it easier for him to torment and kill her later, but the things he'd found had made him feel closer to her, appreciating the strength that she had to possess in order to get to where she was today in spite of her past.

Paige had taken a spot in him that seemed both private and special. It meant that Adam wanted to toy with her far more, to help her and hurt her all at once. He wanted to explore that connection between them, even as he wanted to use all the information that he'd gained to make her life more difficult.

He wanted to explore all the ways that they were similar.

Adam wanted all of that, but there wasn't space in his heart for two women like that. Sara had been special to him for so long, but now it was Paige who was special.

That meant that Adam had felt his feelings towards Sara shifting. He'd hated her for leaving him, but never felt as though he could hurt her. Now, though, with Paige at the center of his attention, he felt as if he could do anything. Sara wasn't protected anymore.

Adam would see Paige soon, would move on to the next phase of the plan he'd been putting together almost since their first session together. But first...

...first, he needed to finish things with Sara. He needed to bring their long, long connection to an end, in the most final way possible.

CHAPTER ELEVEN

Paige had never been inside an FBI office before. It was a far cry from the small, cramped police department she'd been to before, after her father's death, let alone the institutional feel of the places that she worked in as a psychologist.

The building had a marble floor and a huge lobby that reminded Paige of an upscale hotel rather than the place where federal agents carried out their duties. The people walking by wore suits rather than uniforms, making it hard to guess which of them were agents like Christopher and which were support staff. It all felt very orderly compared to a police station, too. This wasn't the kind of place that saw screaming drunks brought in. The crimes it investigated were bigger, and while they caused their own ripples, Paige got no sign of them in the reception area.

Christopher led her to a reception desk to get ID, then up a couple of flights of stairs to his office. That office took up a corner of the building, had a view of the city from a dozen tall windows, and was furnished in rich wooden tones. Paige kept waiting for Christopher to tell her that there'd been some kind of mistake, because it seemed like the kind of place someone far more important might have been given.

In spite of the décor, the office wasn't large, and there was a sense of clutter to it, as if Christopher had too many things to deal with all at once. There were rows of bookshelves along one wall, and Paige found herself glancing over at the titles, trying to get a sense of the kind of man Christopher was.

Appropriately enough for a man who was part of the BAU, there were plenty of books on psychological profiles and serial killers of the past. There were also field manuals, and a few reference books, mostly on legal procedure. They were all neatly shelved in what appeared to be alphabetical order. That said to Paige that Christopher was a man who liked to do things correctly, and who didn't like to cut corners. It also made her wonder about the current clutter in the rest of his office.

"Please excuse the mess," he said, obviously seeing Paige looking around. "It's just, with this landing on my plate so suddenly, there has

69

been no time to deal with anything else. Catching Adam Riker takes priority even over getting things in order."

"You like having things in order?" Paige asked, glad that her guess about him had come through, even if her one about Adam hadn't.

Christopher offered her a smile. "Who doesn't, but we're not here to profile me."

That was a fair point. They were there to try to catch a killer. Even so, Paige couldn't help asking the obvious question.

"Do *you* do a lot of profiling?" She gave the books on the subject a pointed glance. If Christopher was a profiler himself, then why did he need her around?

"Oh, those aren't so I can profile anyone myself," Christopher said, with an amused look. "Those are so that I can understand half the reports that cross my desk from the actual profilers."

Paige had the feeling that he was being too modest, but she was willing to let that go.

"So why the BAU?" she asked. "Why here, if that's not your skillset?"

She saw Christopher shrug. "It's a chance to catch the worst of the worst, often in situations where we don't have a lot of physical evidence to go on initially. The work we do helps us catch killers who otherwise might go on to hurt many more people."

The way that Adam had killed Eloise Harper. The way he might go on to kill other people if they didn't stop him. If *she* didn't stop him.

The strength of that thought caught Paige by surprise. She was just a psychologist who had worked with Adam. It wasn't her responsibility to catch him. That was down to the FBI, to people like Christopher. Paige tried to tell herself that none of this was her fault.

Yet Paige couldn't help feeling a flash of guilt about the way Adam had gotten out, and of fear that he'd learned so much about her. What if he decided to stalk her? What if he decided, after Eloise, that Paige was the next piece of unfinished business he needed to take care of? She even felt guilty for guessing so badly about where Adam was going to try to hide out.

"This is going to be ok," Christopher said, obviously spotting some of her worry. "We're going to catch him."

"We struck out on the farm," Paige replied. She balled her hands into fists at that thought. "*I* struck out."

She'd wasted both of their time with something that she'd half remembered, assuming that Adam was just going to blunder back to his bolt hole, forgetting that he'd told Paige all about it. Of course, Adam was also going to remember that he'd mentioned it in one of his sessions. Of course, he was going to go somewhere else rather than letting himself be caught so easily. Paige had treated him like he was stupid, and it had left them another step behind him.

"Don't be so hard on yourself," Christopher said. "You provided me with a solid lead. It just didn't pan out. At the very least, it means that we'll be able to monitor the old house now, making sure that he doesn't come back. The one thing that I *am* worried about is that you didn't stay put when I told you to wait behind when I was chasing the guy."

"I had to help," Paige said. "Otherwise, I'm not sure what I'm doing here."

Christopher stood up then. "You *are* helping. You're providing me with information about Adam Riker that I couldn't get anywhere else."

"But I could do that from anywhere."

"Not if you can't see what's happening on the ground. Are you telling me that you want to go home, Paige?"

Paige hesitated. *Was* that what she wanted? No, she couldn't, not when Adam was still out there. If she sat back and did nothing, and then he killed again, she would feel as if it were her fault, not just his.

Besides, with Adam still out there, Paige felt as if the safest place to be was right at Christopher's side. Not at home, just waiting for Adam to come for her.

"No, I don't. I'm just surprised you're not off pursuing some other lead, rather than spending your time going around with me, following my guesses about where Adam might be. I can't be your best shot at this."

"We don't have other leads," Christopher said. He waved a hand dismissively. "Oh, I've got local police and state troopers out looking for Adam, and there are lines people can call to report a sighting, but we both know that he's too clever to be caught that way. If that were going to happen, it would have already."

Paige knew that he was right, that Adam was unlikely to be caught by conventional means. He'd only been caught the first time by accident. It would take something special for them to find him now.

"Our best chance of catching him is if someone who knows him can work out where he's going to be next. And no one knows him better than you do, Paige. You're our best chance of finding him."

71

A day or two ago, Paige might have agreed with that statement. Adam was the topic of her PhD thesis, after all. She had dozens of hours of interview recordings of him. She'd written whole chapters on his possible motivations, and on the ways that he'd chosen to work, specifically in the hope of understanding other serial killers.

Like the one who killed her father.

If Paige discovered that she didn't know Adam as well as she thought, then what would that say about her attempts to understand, to find, the man who had killed the one person who had meant more in her life than anybody else? What did it say about anything else she thought she knew?

Until Adam broke out, Paige thought that she knew so much. Now, it felt as if she couldn't be certain about any of it.

"Would you like coffee?" Christopher asked. It seemed like a complete non-sequitur given everything that had gone before.

"Coffee?"

"I'm going to get coffee. If you're going to take another run at this, then I might as well do that while you're working."

"So you just wait for me to give you a direction, then charge off that way after Adam? Is that how FBI agents work?"

"When they have experts that they can rely on, yes," Christopher said. "Now, coffee?"

Paige nodded. "Coffee would be good."

Christopher's attempts to just do something normal helped. It gave Paige some space to think. She *was* going to take another run at this, and this time, she was determined to do things better. She was going to find an answer that would let her locate Adam and actually finish this.

That meant delving back into her research. Paige opened up her laptop and started to look through the files again, trying to work out where else Adam might go. His first murder since his escape might provide a clue to what he was thinking at the moment, Paige guessed. After all, he'd gone after someone who he'd intended to make his victim previously. Did that tell her anything about what he was trying to do now that he was out, and what he intended to do next?

Paige didn't think he was just working through a list of escaped victims. As far as Paige knew, Eloise Harper had been the only person to actually get away from Adam once he'd begun his hunt for them. Paige didn't want to just rely on her memory though, so she started to run word searches through her files, searching for any mention of victims, or people Adam intended to make his victim.

Paige found a passage in her transcripts that intrigued her.

"I suppose you want me to talk about my first victims and what they meant to me. About how those shaped me. Shall I tell you about when I killed my father? About how he deserved it after years of abusing me, trying to beat the evil out of me?"

Something about that struck a note with Paige, and not just because of her own experiences at the hands of her stepfather. Those weren't the same thing. They weren't. Paige's experiences were her own. They had nothing to do with Adam or what he'd been through. The two of them weren't the same.

But it started her thinking about what he'd told her of his situation. His father was abusive, his mother left, forced out by his father. His uncle had apparently known about it all, and even helped his father with some of the worst of it. Adam had hated him for it, almost as much as the father he'd killed.

At the time, it had all seemed like a vital part of trying to understand why Adam was the way he was, but it hadn't seemed like a sufficient explanation. After all, Paige had been through as much as Adam, maybe more, but she hadn't turned out to be a serial killer. She wanted to help people and catch men like him, not kill people herself. She'd taken it as proof that there was some other element involved, something she might be able to get to, if she only put in enough work.

Now, though, thinking about Adam's uncle made Paige want to go back to those sections of her notes. It didn't take long to find his name: George Riker. It turned out that Paige hadn't looked up much more about him than that. She seemed to recall that, briefly, she'd considered the possibility of interviewing him about Adam's past, but Paige had wanted to keep her work focused on the sessions, not run off interviewing random strangers who had no reason to talk to her. Her work had been about the dynamic between the two of them, not about what other people thought.

In that moment, Paige considered Adam's motivations for killing Eloise Harper. That had been about completing unfinished business, about gaining, she guessed, a kind of closure about his arrest in his own sick and twisted way.

Adam might not have other victims he'd failed to kill, but this was definitely unfinished business, definitely something that Adam might want to find a kind of closure about.

Christopher came back in carrying two mugs of coffee. He took one look at Paige's expression and stopped short.

73

"You've found something?"

"I think so," Paige said. "The first killing seems to have been about a sense of things left incomplete, right?"

She saw Christopher nod in response to that. "I guess so."

"Well, there's something else in his life that is definitely incomplete. He killed his father because of the abuse he suffered at his father's hands."

"That sounds pretty final to me," Christopher said, but he hadn't heard the rest of it yet.

"Except that his father isn't the only person Adam blames," Paige explained. "He said in his sessions that his uncle, George Riker, played a part too. That they were both to blame for driving his mother away. As far as I'm aware, George Riker is still alive, and that might make him someone Adam might want to get to, now that he's free."

"So we need to get to George Riker before his nephew does," Christopher said.

Paige nodded. "Only I don't know where he is. I never looked into him for my research."

"I can check with the DMV," Christopher said. "I should be able to get an address, too. This is good work, Paige."

Paige felt a surge of pride at those words, especially coming from Christopher. Paige found that she wanted to find ways to impress him. Meanwhile, he was already on his phone.

"This is Agent Marriott with the FBI. I'm looking for a current address for a George Riker. Yes, it's in connection with that. Yes, I'll wait a moment." He stood there for a few seconds. "That's great. You're sure it's the right George Riker? Thank you."

He hung up and turned to Paige.

"You're convinced that Riker is going to try to kill his uncle?"

Paige nodded. "I am."

"Then I'd better get over there before he does."

CHAPTER TWELVE

They set off, taking Christopher's car.

"I'd feel more comfortable if you stayed behind," Christopher said, driving quickly along the streets of D.C.

"I think it will be better if I'm there," Paige argued. "I've been involved in this whole thing, and I know more about Adam than anyone else does. Maybe I'll spot something that you don't, because it fits with something in my research."

Paige wasn't sure what she could see that Christopher wouldn't, especially when they were mostly just going to make sure that Adam's uncle was safe. Christopher was the field agent here. She was just a psychologist who had gotten caught up in it all. Yet she felt certain that there would be some opportunity to help here.

"All right, but don't take any risks," Christopher said, continuing to drive. "So, why exactly do you think that he'll go after his uncle?"

Paige shrugged. "It fits. I mean, Adam's father is dead. His mother is gone, probably dead. There's no one else in his family that he could have had a relationship with. His uncle is the only family he has left. And he hates him."

At least according to the files. There was another aspect to that too.

"So does he have any relationship with his uncle at this point?" Christopher asked, touching on it.

"Adam says that their relationship was abusive," Paige said. "His uncle was another figure who he blamed for everything that had gone wrong with his life. In his sessions, he said that his father beat him, and his uncle helped. That he was part of driving Adam's mother away. I think he blamed him more for that than for all the rest of it."

They approached the edge of the city, with rows of older houses that had been subdivided into apartments. According to the address, the next street was where Adam's uncle lived. It was the kind of place that had probably once been intended to be some bright, clean development, but it had never quite worked out like that.

Given the location, Paige hadn't been expecting a mansion, but the house that they pulled up to was fairly modest even by the standards of her expectations. It was a single-story, with a driveway and a garage off to one side.

They pulled up in front of it, and Christopher got out and approached the front door. Paige followed him up the front steps, standing beside him as he knocked on the door.

"Hello?" he called out. "Mr. Riker?"

There was no reply initially, and Christopher called out again.

"Mr. Riker, it's the FBI."

Now, Paige heard someone coming.

The door opened, and a man in his late fifties stood before them. He had a weather-beaten face, with lines around his eyes, and gray hair that looked as if it hadn't been combed for days. His eyes were bloodshot, but Paige felt as though she could see a hint of Adam's features in his. This was definitely his uncle.

"What do you want?" he asked.

"I'm Agent Marriott, with the FBI," Christopher said, holding up his ID for the other man to look over.

"So what?" the uncle asked. "You think that's gonna make a difference here? I don't care who you are. You got no right to be bothering me."

"If I could just ask you a couple of questions, sir," Christopher said. "It's about your nephew."

Paige saw the older man's expression sour even more. She hadn't been sure that was even possible.

"Adam's been dead to me for years," he said. "I have no interest in talking about him. After the things he's done, you think he matters anymore? You think that whatever happened to him matters to me?"

Paige saw the man's hands balling into fists at the thought of his nephew, but Paige knew they needed to ignore him. If she could just get him to listen, she might be able to keep him from making a mistake.

"Do you know where your nephew might be?" Christopher asked. That was the question that mattered here. "He escaped from the facility holding him."

"Well... shit," George Riker said, looking genuinely surprised. Obviously he hadn't been watching the news.

"You must have some idea of where he might go."

"I won't tell you anything," the uncle said. "Not until you tell me more about what's going on. You could have sent local police to ask me if I'd seen Adam. You didn't drive all the way out here just to ask me that."

"We have reason to believe that your nephew might be planning to do something," Christopher said. "Something dangerous. Something to you."

Paige saw the surprise on George Riker's face, and that caught *her* by surprise. Did he really not think that his serial killer nephew might want to hurt him? After everything he'd done, did he really think that there was no reason Adam might want to kill him?

"You better come in," the older man said. "I've got nothing to hide."

The older man led them into the house. As they entered, the interior caught Paige by surprise. The smell of cigarettes and sweat hung in the air. It was a dingy place, with dark décor and a sense of uncleanliness that set Paige's teeth on edge.

"I want to know what you're doing here," George Riker said.

He led the way through to a lounge that was as dirty as the rest of the place. He pointed to Christopher as Paige took a seat on the cleanest piece of furniture she could find.

"I want to know what you're doing here, and I want to know how you found me."

"The information's out there, for anyone who looks for it," Christopher said. "For Adam, if he tries to find it."

"And you think that my nephew is going to use that to come looking for me? You think he's going to risk his freedom by coming after me, rather than running while he has the chance?"

Paige nodded. "We do. He hates you, Mr. Riker."

"You're crazy," George Riker said. Again, he had a look of surprise that Paige found hard to believe. He had to know all the reasons that Adam hated him. "My own nephew wouldn't do anything like that. Not to me. Adam's not coming here. He's never been in touch with me. You're just trying to frighten me, and I won't stand for it."

"He escaped from a secure psychiatric institution yesterday," Christopher pointed out. "Since then, he has killed already, murdering the woman who was going to be his victim when he was caught last time. He's finishing up old business."

"That still doesn't mean that he's coming for me," George Riker said. "Why would it?"

Paige couldn't help the surprise that she felt as he said that. George Riker seemed so sure that this had nothing to do with him. "Are you sure of that?"

"I know Adam," George Riker said, and there was a depth of emotion behind those words. "Whatever he might have done, there's no way that he would do anything like that. I know my nephew."

"I don't think he shares the same feelings," Paige said. "He pointedly told us that he hated you and blamed you for everything that happened in his life."

"He said that he hated me?" George Riker asked. He looked a little taken aback by that. "I thought he blamed his father."

"He blamed you too," Paige said. "The abuse that he suffered, the way you helped your brother hurt him. He said that you were part of it all."

George Riker looked truly shocked now. Then he shook his head.

"What are you talking about? That's not what happened. That's not even close to it."

Not what happened? That didn't make any kind of sense. Paige had detailed descriptions of what had taken place down in the transcripts of her sessions with Adam. She had recordings of Adam telling her exactly what part George Riker had played in all of it.

"It's what he said in his sessions," Paige countered. "He said that you forced his mother out."

"But it's not right," the older man said. "It's not what happened. When his mother left, the only one he should have blamed was himself, not his father. Not me."

"And why were you in the house when he got hurt?" Paige pushed. She wasn't about to just let this go, even though it should have been Christopher's job to ask the questions here. "You helped your brother beat him, didn't you?"

"I never did anything like that," George Riker snapped back, obviously angered by the accusation. He looked at Christopher. "Anything that you've heard, anything that my nephew said. It wasn't true. It was just more lies, more of the things that he said to get whatever he wanted."

Paige frowned. "Then why did he say these things? Why did he tell me this in the middle of his therapy sessions?"

"I never beat him," George Riker said adamantly. "I never touched him. I never did anything but try to help Adam. But he was wild, out of control. He used to hurt other kids, and he'd have the strangest look on his face. He never listened. All I ever tried to do was get him some help. I tried to get him to talk to a shrink, but he just refused, even sat there in a session and said nothing for the whole hour, just staring."

The same way that he'd refused to talk during his first session with Paige. Adam had just sat there the first time they'd met, refusing to speak, so that she'd thought that she was wasting her time. Yet for some reason, this serial killer had opened up to her. He'd seen something in her, or decided that he wanted something from her, that had made him talk.

It made Paige wonder about her own instincts at work.

"I tried everything I could for Adam," George Riker said. "I tried to help him. I even tried to get the police to help him. I thought if they intervened early, it might stop him from going further. I didn't hurt him. He has no reason to want to kill me."

"Is there anything at all that you can remember that might have caused him to hate you?" Paige asked. There had to be something, some reason that Adam had said what he did.

"No, nothing," George replied. "I think this is all some big mistake."

Christopher was shaking his head, though. "It doesn't matter if you can't think of a reason why he would want to hurt you. All that matters is that Adam *can*, even if that reason is only in his head. He's broken out of the institution that was holding him, and he might be coming for you, Mr. Riker."

Paige saw the older man swallow at the thought of that. He wasn't in denial about this part, at least. He obviously knew exactly what his nephew was capable of. He must have read the news about the killings.

At last, he seemed to be taking the threat that Adam posed to him seriously.

"So what do you suggest?" George asked.

Christopher gestured to the car. "Now you have a choice, sir. Option one is that we take you into protective custody until all of this is over."

George didn't look happy about that option. "And option two?"

"You stay here," Christopher said.

George Riker's eyes widened. "But that would be crazy. What if he does come here? I'd be sitting here, just waiting for him to kill me."

"And we'd be waiting too," Christopher said. "Ready to intercept him the moment that he attempts to do so."

"You want to use me as bait?" George Riker asked incredulously. "You want me to sit here and wait for my nephew to come here and kill me?"

79

Christopher nodded. "It's the best way for us to catch him, sir. We want to stop him from coming for you, but we can't catch him without your help. I know I'm asking you to take a risk, but it's one that could save lives."

George Riker looked from Christopher to Paige, then back again. "So… my only choice in all of this is to be bait?"

Paige bit her lip. There was something sickening about the whole idea. But Christopher was right. They needed this man, if they were going to catch Adam.

"I'm sorry," Paige said. "But I think it's the only option."

George Riker asked. "You think that's a good idea?"

"It's better than anything else that we have," Paige said. "It gives us a chance of actually stopping Adam, and if we don't, he could, he *will* just keep killing people."

Paige saw her words hit home with George Riker, who sat there staring at her. After several seconds, he looked over at Christopher.

"What are you going to do if he comes?"

Christopher looked determined, and when he spoke, it was in an obviously reassuring tone. "We'll be waiting. I'll have a whole team watching the house, and we'll arrest him before he gets anywhere near you."

George Riker nodded. "I understand. If it's the only way to catch my nephew, then that's what I'll have to do."

CHAPTER THIRTEEN

Sara Langdon normally liked to work late at the office, often going several hours beyond any of her colleagues. It meant that she had the place to herself after everyone else had gone home, and she could get things done without any distractions.

Working late was also a big part of her role as a junior partner in the business. She was as responsible for its successes and failures as anyone now; but she didn't have the cushion of years of service that the senior partners enjoyed. She couldn't just clock off the way a normal employee might. She had to be here late, if she was going to have any hope of getting her work done.

She couldn't really afford to have anyone else in here with her, either. The whole point of this was that she could get her work done in peace.

But tonight, Sara had her own problems to deal with. She had a presentation due tomorrow, and if it didn't go well, then the whole Florida deal was likely to go badly. She had gotten into the office early enough, and she had planned to only work until seven. It was already seven fifteen, and she was still barely a quarter of the way through everything she needed to get done. At this rate, it was going to be past midnight before she was finished with it all.

She was far too distracted. Maybe some of the distraction was down to the news that Adam Riker had escaped from prison. Sara had known Adam, back when they'd both been teenagers, and Sara had been kind of wild. She'd even gone out with him, for a while, before they both decided to break things off.

He had been a bad boy, a little older than her, and he'd had a whole host of issues that she never really understood. Even then, she had known that he was just the sort of guy that she needed to stay away from, but he had been so charming, and he had pursued her so relentlessly that she had given in, after a while.

It had only lasted a couple of months, though. She'd tried to keep up with him, tried to go along with all his crazy ideas. She'd thought that he would be fun, but in the end, he'd just been too much for her.

She'd seen the darkness in him. Some days, Sara found herself wondering if, had she told someone about him earlier, they might have been able to stop him before he hurt anyone. She wondered if she had some kind of responsibility for what he'd done.

But what could she have said? She couldn't have predicted what he would do. The young man she had known back then had his problems but was nothing like the killer that he had become.

He was out now, though, and that was the thought that had consumed her ever since she heard the news. She glanced at her watch. It was almost half past seven. She was tired and she still had plenty of work left to do. She needed to finish up on these accounts, and then she needed to get home and get a good night's sleep.

She was still trying to work when she heard the sound of a footstep, somewhere behind her. Sara turned, ready to deal with whatever this was.

"I didn't realize that there was anyone still in the office. Did you need-"

Adam was standing right in front of her, wearing dark clothes, just standing waiting, as if her thoughts had conjured him.

Sara froze in place. She knew that she should try to get to something she could use as a weapon, or try to run, but in that moment, she couldn't bring herself to even begin to move.

She looked at the man in front of her. He was staring straight at her with those cold, dead eyes that she'd seen before, the last time she'd been with him. It was those eyes, more than all the rest of it that had made her break up with him, running as far as she could.

She had heard what he'd done, but she couldn't quite believe that it was Adam there in front of her. He looked different now. He looked like a stranger.

"Adam?"

He was right in front of her, right in front of where she was standing in front of her desk. A few more steps and he would be level with her.

"This is crazy," she said. "You can't be here like this. When you broke out, I thought you'd run. What are you doing here?"

She tried to reason with him. She wasn't sure what she was hoping for. A simple apology, maybe, or a promise that he wouldn't hurt her.

Instead, he just kept walking towards her, until he was just a few feet away from where she was standing.

"Adam, you need to talk to me. What are you doing here?"

"Do you need to ask, after everything you did to me?" Adam replied. He had a bag in his left hand. From it, he took a pair of handcuffs and tossed them onto her desk. "Put these on. Don't try calling for help. There's no one else in the building to hear you."

"You don't have to do this," Sara said. He couldn't do this. But she was beginning to think that she was wrong. Adam was serious. She could tell from how calm he was being. There was a coldness to the way he spoke that said that there was no reasoning with him.

She didn't want to put the handcuffs on. She knew what would happen if she did. This whole situation made her so afraid that it was making her sick. She only had to look into Adam's eyes to know that he was going to kill her.

She looked over at the closed door. He had said that he was the only one here. There was no one else there to help her. That meant that Sara had to deal with this herself. She needed to remember that she wasn't helpless. She needed to get out of here.

"Why are you doing this?" she asked, edging towards the door. If she could get close enough, she might be able to run.

"You know! You know what you did!"

He stepped forward, striking her hard and sending her spinning to the floor.

Sara tried to fight. She wasn't about to give up that easily. She kicked out at him, catching him in the thigh.

He struck back at her, and Sara managed to avoid the first blow, but a second caught her in the stomach. Sara fought back through the pain, slamming her forehead into his face. She might work in an office now, but she remembered how to fight.

It bought her a moment of space, but only a moment. Adam was on her in an instant, grappling, trying to use his size and weight advantage. The two of them slammed into the desk, knocking it aside.

Sara went for Adam's eyes with outstretched fingers, but he dodged aside from that, picking her up and slamming her to the floor. That knocked the breath from Sara, but still she tried to turn and struggle to her feet.

Adam didn't need another opportunity. His weight was on her then, holding her in place while he wrenched Sara's hands behind her back and cuffed them in place. His weight held her there, even as she tried to break free from him.

"You know exactly what you did," Adam said. "You thought that you could just throw me away, like I was nothing to you. But I'm not just going to forget all that you did to me. All the pain that you put me through, you're going to get it in return."

"It wasn't like that," Sara said.

"It's exactly like that," Adam said. "You thought you were better than me, and you threw me aside like I was a piece of garbage."

That wasn't how Sara remembered any of it. She remembered a dangerous young man who had frightened her until she hadn't been able to stay close to him any longer. She tried to struggle as Adam started to take things from his bag: lengths of rope, a knife that gleamed by the office light. He just grabbed her and held her in place.

"That's not what happened, Adam," Sara said, trying to reason with him, while at the same time trying to find a way out of the bonds that held her. She tried to keep the fear out of her voice and failed utterly. "We drifted apart. It wasn't my fault, and it wasn't your fault. It just happened."

"It wasn't my fault?" Adam said. "No, you're the only one who's to blame for all of this."

Sara wanted to head for the door. She wanted to fight her way out of there. But Adam was holding her too tightly for her to get her feet under her.

"We just... Things weren't working out between us."

"That's not how I remember it," Adam said. "I remember you telling me that you were sick of me. You told me that I didn't care about you, and you were right. I didn't care. I didn't care about you being with him. I didn't care about you leaving me. I didn't care about what you did."

"Adam, please-"

"Shut up," Adam said. "You don't get to tell me what to do. You're not my girlfriend anymore. You're not my anything. You aren't special anymore, Sara."

Sara knew in that moment that she was going to die, but she had to try something. She had to try to find some way to get through to Adam.

"I've read about the things you did," she said. "You were killing people right after you were with me, but you didn't come for me before. You didn't try to hurt me back then."

"That was a mistake," Adam said. He started to work with the ropes from the bag, wrenching Sara's body this way and that as he tied her in a position that seemed impossible to hold. That hurt her just being there. Her arms were wrenched high behind her, the pressure on her shoulders making it an effort to breathe.

84

"I don't think it *was* a mistake," Sara said. "I think you didn't hurt me because some part of you still loved me. I think you still love me now. I don't think you want to do this. I just think you want to be close to me."

Adam laughed then, and there was something cruel about the emptiness of that laugh.

"That might even have been true, once," he said. "There was a time when you were my whole world. I longed to be close to you, to touch you. I would have done anything for you."

"Then do something for me now," Sara begged. "Let me go."

"No."

There was a finality to that word that made Sara shiver.

"I've found someone new," Adam said. "Someone better. Someone who *deserves* my attention. You... I'm going to stand here and watch until you run out of the strength to hold that posture. Until your body starts to suffocate itself. Can you feel it, Sara?"

Sara could, each breath taking more effort than the last.

"Please, Adam," she begged, as if that might make some kind of difference.

Adam just stood there, watching her coldly as she grew weaker, little by little...

"And to speed things along, a little," Adam said. "Let's give you some incentive to move."

He had a knife in his hand then. Sara wanted to get away from him, wanted to struggle and fight, but she couldn't do anything as he brought it up to make the first cut...

CHAPTER FOURTEEN

Paige sat with Christopher in his car, parked opposite George Riker's home, both of them trying to keep low and out of sight as they waited for Adam Riker to come to get his revenge on his uncle.

They weren't alone for this one. Christopher had called in a team from the FBI field office; they were out there too, in cars or on foot, waiting for the moment when Adam arrived, and they would strike, moving to arrest him.

"We need to take him down as soon as possible," Christopher said. "The moment he shows his face, we arrest him. We can't afford to let him get inside and risk turning this into a hostage situation."

It was a fine theory. Paige hoped that it would work out like that. If Adam showed up, she hoped that the FBI would be able to get to him before he could hurt anyone else. Not George Riker, and not her.

There was no sign of Adam yet, though. The sun had set by now. Paige checked her phone for the time and realized that she had been waiting there for hours.

"Is this what your work is usually like?" Paige asked.

"What? Sitting around waiting for a serial killer to show up?" Christopher replied, with a faint smile. "Not usually."

Paige smiled too, relieving some of the tension that was getting to them, even though neither of them would ever admit it.

"Yeah. I have to say," Paige said. "This is really not quite what I expected. I kinda thought you'd be out there chasing killers all over the city. Not sitting still waiting for one."

"Well, yes," Christopher said. "Chases happen, but usually only if we get something wrong. It's better if we contain them and don't give them a chance to run."

"I guess I was just thinking of the things I'd seen in cop shows," Paige said. "I don't know. I guess the idea of the FBI is a little bit different from the reality."

"Really?" Christopher said, shaking his head. "It's not like that. We don't shoot all the bad guys, or save all the pretty girls, or take down all the serial killers in one-on-one battles that we barely survive. It's not like the movies."

Which was a pity in one way, because right then, Paige could have done with some action to alleviate the boredom of the stakeout. Her legs felt as though they'd fallen asleep an hour ago. What was she even doing on a stakeout? She was just a psych grad-student, not an FBI field agent.

Time wore on slowly with nothing to do but to sit and watch the house. The fact that doing so was literally the point of her being there didn't make it easier. The neighborhood was quiet and peaceful, but the tension in the air was palpable. Paige hated to think of what George Riker's neighbors would think if they saw a bunch of suspicious-looking men hanging around, and called the cops, not realizing that the FBI was already there.

"Do you think he'll come?" Paige asked.

"I don't know," Christopher said. "This is your lead, Paige."

That sounded too much as if he were distancing himself from the idea, at least until Christopher went on.

"But I trust your judgement. And if he does, we're going to be ready for it. You'll see."

There was very little to do, unless Paige counted watching the lights on Christopher's dashboard. She sat there, trying to persuade herself that sooner or later, Adam would show up.

He didn't. The neighborhood stayed quiet and dark, the only sounds the usual ones of nearby traffic. Even Christopher seemed to be getting twitchy, shifting in his seat as he waited for the action to come.

They both reacted as a call came through on his phone, the sound of it sudden against the silence of the car. Paige almost jumped with fright in her seat. Christopher answered instantly.

"What?" he barked, obviously not happy about being disturbed like that when they were meant to be lying in wait for Adam.

Paige could hear the voice of someone from FBI headquarters over the phone. It sounded as though they were speaking very quickly, but she couldn't understand what they were saying.

Christopher's eyes flicked towards Paige as he continued the conversation. He looked uncertain as he kept going.

"Are you sure?" he said.

Paige wished that she could hear the other end of the conversation, but she wasn't going to get that chance.

"All right. We'll be right over."

Christopher hung up, then he shook his head, looking suddenly and utterly dejected.

"We're in the wrong place," he said. "We've brought the teams here for nothing."

Paige frowned at that. "How do you know?"

"Because there has been another murder, and it isn't Riker's uncle. A woman has been killed in an office building downtown."

*

Paige followed Christopher into the office building, trying to hold back the waves of disappointment at being wrong. The two of them were moving quickly. Paige felt as though her head was spinning with the speed that things were happening. They'd gone from parked outside George Riker's house to heading for this place in a matter of minutes, obviously racing to catch up with what Adam had done now in the hopes that, if they were quick enough, they might be able to keep up with him and find him.

The building was a tall block on the edge of Constitution Avenue. There were police waiting at the entrance, who let the two of them in as they approached. Inside, it seemed to Paige just like any other office building in D.C., with dark corridors and offices running in lines down the length of the building. They walked past a number of people as they went, all police or emergency responders, but Christopher didn't seem to care about that. He was all business.

"Which way?" he asked a local police officer guarding one of the stairwells.

"Just up those stairs, second on the right," the officer replied as Christopher flashed his ID. "Who's the woman?"

"Paige King. She's with me."

He didn't say anything else before he set off up the stairs. In fact, he'd been pretty quiet since the news had broken that they were in the wrong place.

Paige could barely keep up as Christopher led the way up the stairs to the second floor and turned right. She didn't really understand what was going on, had never seen so many cops in one place before. Yes, she'd attended the crime scene at Adam's last kill, but that had felt as though it was winding down, with half the cops standing around looking bored. This was something different, something fresh. She ignored the looks that she got from the others, just trying to keep up.

They reached a door with a police officer standing guard on it. He stepped out of the way when Christopher flashed his ID again, and Paige followed the FBI agent into the room beyond without thinking.

She found herself staring at a body.

The body of a woman was strung up among a web of ropes, hanging like a fly in a spider's web.

"We should have been here," Christopher said, in a voice filled with tension. "We should have been able to stop there being another victim."

He was right, and the guilt at that failure filled Paige instantly. This was her fault. She'd been so *certain*.

Paige could see the signs of torture on the woman's body, the bruises and cuts that marked her flesh. This was nothing like a crime scene photograph. This was far more visceral. Far more like... like looking down at her father's corpse, all over again. She didn't look too closely; the sight was too much.

That made her miss a step. She only just managed to catch herself, but the FBI agent noticed, taking hold of her arm to support her, as if worried that she might faint at the sight. Paige wanted to tell him that she was made of sterner stuff, but she wasn't sure that it was true, right then.

"Are you okay?" Christopher asked.

Paige shook her head, trying to clear her mind of the disturbing sight. "No. No, I'm not."

Paige had spent her days interviewing serial killers. Interviewing Adam. She'd thought that she understood him, but here, looking at his handiwork, Paige knew that she hadn't really understood at all. She'd treated the whole thing as some kind of intellectual exercise, a puzzle to unpick, but there was a woman, body contorted impossibly, left hanging there while forensics officers worked to gather any evidence they could.

The sight of her there sickened Paige, and it was only made worse by the fact that her wrong guess had made this possible.

"Hey," Christopher said to her, trying to catch her attention. "Are you all right?"

"I will be," Paige said. "Just give me a minute."

She blinked, trying to clear her eyes and her mind. She hadn't expected to be so affected, but there was a human being down there, a woman, a human being that had been strung up and tortured to death. It was shocking, and Paige found herself breathing heavily and trying to calm down.

She took a few deep, calming breaths. Then she nodded, gesturing for Christopher to continue.

"Okay," she said. "I'm ready."

"Are you sure?" Christopher asked.

Paige managed to nod, and Christopher gestured to one of the techs there at the scene, dressed in a full evidence suit and mask.

"Donna, what do we have?"

The tech glanced up at the body, then back at Christopher and Paige.

"This is Sara Langdon. She died probably less than an hour ago. We'll need to do a full autopsy to determine cause of death..."

"Heart failure," Paige interrupted. "Or suffocation. She died from positional asphyxia while being tortured."

The tech gave Paige a strange look, but then nodded. "We're taking samples and photographs now. We'll get them to the lab as quickly as possible and we'll know more then. But that's the preliminary."

Paige knew how she'd died, because Adam had been very detailed in his descriptions of what he'd done to his victims.

"Paige," Christopher said, looking from her to the victim. "Who is this woman?"

"I...," Paige wracked her brain for an answer to that question, but finally had to admit the truth. "I don't know. Her name sounds familiar, but I don't know why. I don't know who she is, or why Adam did this. I was so *sure* that he was going to go after his uncle."

Instead, he'd gone after some woman Paige hadn't heard of, and Paige didn't know why. In spite of the horror that she felt at being there in the middle of a crime scene, she got out her laptop. She had to check her notes. Maybe there would be some kind of answers in there.

She had to know the truth.

CHAPTER FIFTEEN

Christopher looked around the crime scene, trying to get a better sense of what had happened. Not so that they could find out who had done this. As with the crime scene before this one, they knew that part, but in case there was anything that might lead to the killer.

"It's hard to tell if there was a struggle, based on the damage to the victim," Donna the forensic tech said. "We'll only know for sure after the autopsy. My guess is he threatened her to get her into this position before he started... work."

Based on what he could see in the office, Christopher wasn't so sure about that.

"See the mark there, on the carpet?" he said. "Where the table has been standing?"

"Yes?"

"Well, what made it move?" Christopher asked. "I think he grabbed for her, or hit her, when she was close to the desk. She must have stumbled against it and knocked it out of place."

"True. So we should be able to get prints and DNA."

"What about the ropes?" he asked. "Do they match the ones found at the other crime scene?"

"They do," Donna confirmed. "Same manufacturer. We've got some matching fibers from the earlier crime scene, but we can't yet confirm that this is the same rope."

Not that any of it mattered. They were all still looking at this the way they would look at a normal crime scene, the way they'd been trained to look. They were all searching for evidence of the killer's identity, but when they already knew that, it didn't help to get them closer to catching him.

Maybe the ropes might help? If Riker favored a single type, then it might be possible to track any new purchases. That was a long shot though, and Christopher knew it.

Christopher wanted to tear the room apart, find some clue that would help them find Adam, but he knew that wouldn't work. It wouldn't be in there. The physical clues simply weren't enough to help him catch Riker.

His best hope of catching the serial killer was the psychologist who currently stood in the middle of the murder scene, going through her laptop as if all the answers lay in there. As if it were simultaneously her comfort blanket to grip against the sight in front of her and a source of information that she needed to interrogate to work out why it hadn't given her the right answers.

Christopher could only guess at what Paige was feeling, seeing her reaction to what had happened, but he could only imagine that it was a lot worse than he felt. He'd been to his fair share of crime scenes but seeing what had happened to Sara Langdon was disturbing. Seeing how she'd died was disturbing.

For Paige, there had to be whole other levels to it, with the sight of the dead woman in front of her and the realization that her understanding of the killer's motivation was wrong, it had to be. She had to be questioning everything she knew about him.

Was she going to be able to handle this? Christopher hoped so. He needed her.

She'd been so sure that Adam was going after his uncle. That hadn't been the case. He'd gone after another woman.

"I don't know what went wrong," Paige muttered as she looked through her files. "The uncle was the obvious choice."

"That doesn't mean he was the only one," Christopher replied. He could hear the dejection in Paige's voice, the guilt. He knew he'd let too much of his own disappointment show on the way over. He guessed she would take that as a comment on her efforts, when Christopher was really just frustrated that he couldn't seem to stop Adam Riker.

He saw her expression change, a look of surprise coming to her, along with what seemed to be an amplification to the guilt.

"Wait."

He could see that she had new information. "What?"

"I... think I know who Sara Langdon is."

Ok, that was interesting news, as far as Christopher was concerned. "Who is she?"

"Adam mentioned a Sara in one of his sessions. Just once. A former girlfriend. He said that she was wild. That she used to go around committing small crimes with him. That he thought she was like him. That he loved her, and she broke his heart, but he didn't feel as though he could hurt her."

"So what changed?" Christopher asked, with a look back towards where the technicians were just starting to get the body ready to remove it.

"I... I don't know." Paige replied, uncertainty filling her voice again. "I'm sorry."

"Don't be sorry," Christopher said. "You're doing your best."

"And you think it's good enough?"

"I know it's good enough," Christopher replied. "This case is tricky, and you're doing your best to work out what he's doing. This isn't your fault."

"I wish I could believe that," Paige said, and then Christopher saw her pale.

"What is it?"

"Her family name is in the notes. He actually called her Sara Langdon."

Christopher didn't get the significance of that. "So?"

"So I *could* have identified her, based on those notes, if I'd only guessed the significance of that session. We could have found her. If I'd just worked out that she was going to be the next victim, if I'd identified the girl before this, we could have saved her."

Christopher touched her arm. He knew that she needed the reassurance, right then. "You can't blame yourself for this. You did everything you could."

"I feel like I didn't do enough," Paige said.

"You're not a detective, Paige. You're a psychologist. You're doing your best with this. Don't beat yourself up about it."

Even so, he saw her shake her head.

"I just feel like I have to do better."

"I know you do," Christopher replied. "And you're going to. But there's no point in dwelling on what might have happened. We have to deal with what actually happened. We have to catch Adam. And that's going to take some doing."

Paige still looked upset. "We were sitting there, outside George Riker's house, while this woman was being murdered."

"Paige, look at me," Christopher said gently, maintaining the contact of his hand on her arm. "Do you want to stop? You've done your best to help me, but you're not an FBI agent. This isn't your job."

"I... I want to do this," Paige said, and the determination in her voice was impressive.

She looked up at him, and for a moment or two, Christopher couldn't quite place the look on her face. She was looking at him intently, almost as if...

Then his phone rang, breaking the moment even as Christopher started to work out what was going on in it.

Christopher picked up instantly once he saw that it was his wife, Justine.

"Hey Justine," he said, trying to keep his voice light. She deserved better than to see the side of him that worried about whether they were going to be able to catch a killer. "Is everything all right?"

"No, it's not all right," she replied, in a tone of obvious annoyance. "Where are you? I was making dinner tonight, remember?"

"Oh, shit," he said, realizing that he'd completely forgotten. "I'm so sorry Justine. It's just been a really busy couple of days. You saw the news?"

"You know what might have been easier than the news?" Justine said. "If maybe my husband had called me to tell me what was going on."

"I'm sorry," Christopher said. He held back the urge to tell her that he was currently standing in a murder scene. "I... I've been dealing with this case. We got a lead on the serial killer. I've had to move fast to try to catch up to him."

"I get that, Chris," she never called him Chris, "but you could have found the time for one phone call, so I knew you were safe. Running around after killers, do you think I don't worry?"

"I'm sorry, I didn't think," he said, apologetic again.

"No, I guess you didn't. Do you have him? Your serial killer?"

Christopher couldn't even soften this with that piece of good news.

"Not yet," Christopher replied. "We're close."

"Good," Justine replied. "I just... I want you to be safe."

"I will be," Christopher said. "I promise."

"I love you," Justine finished.

"I love you too," Christopher said, replying automatically, and hung up. He caught Paige's questioning look. "My wife, Justine."

"Ah," Paige said, before turning away to look at her computer again. "Congratulations."

She looked... slightly embarrassed for a moment or two, her cheeks reddening, like she didn't know what to say. Christopher wasn't sure what to make of that. He hadn't mentioned his wife to this point, but why would he? It wasn't as if there was anything between him and Paige.

"Look," Christopher said. "It's getting late. I don't think we're going to catch Riker today."

He caught Paige's wince at that. She obviously still thought that this was her fault, rather than just the way cases went. But then, she didn't know that Christopher struck out more often than he didn't. The important thing was to keep going.

"Come on," he said. "I'll give you a ride home."

"That…," for a moment, he thought that she might reject the offer. "That would be good, thanks."

He would give her a ride home, then go back to Justine. He just had to hope that Paige would turn up some good leads for him by tomorrow.

CHAPTER SIXTEEN

Paige couldn't stop thinking about what she'd seen at the crime scene. It wasn't just the sight of the woman tangled there in death. It was what it said about Adam. His coldness, his control, his lack of emotion. He seemed to have no conscience. No humanity, no empathy. He killed women and didn't bat an eyelid. He felt no remorse for his actions.

Paige had known all of that in theory from their sessions but seeing Sara Langdon hanging there dead in a web of ropes was something else entirely. It was a reminder that this wasn't some academic game leading to her thesis; people's lives were in the balance, and when Paige got things wrong, they died for those mistakes.

She should have figured it out. She should have been able to identify Sara as the next victim. Her name had been in Paige's notes, after all, and didn't it make sense that Adam might go after a former girlfriend he felt had slighted him? If she'd spotted all of that, then maybe Christopher would have been there in time to catch Adam. Maybe then, Sara Langdon would still be alive.

Paige tried to tell herself that it wasn't her job to solve all this, that she was just a psychologist caught up in it all, but she kept thinking about Sara's body. She kept seeing her hanging there, with her dead eyes staring at Paige in silent accusation.

And she kept thinking about Christopher, in spite of her best efforts to do anything else.

In the last day or so, Paige had caught a glimpse of a man she really wanted to get to know better. There was something intelligent, determined, kind about Christopher, not to mention the fact he seemed so easily in control of dangerous situations. She wanted to find a way to get close to him, to know him more deeply.

For one brief moment, she'd thought that there might be something more than even that. She'd thought that there might be something between them, but then Christopher's wife had called him, and just the fact that he had a wife had made it clear that getting any closer to him simply wasn't an option. Whatever Paige had thought was growing between them wasn't real. It couldn't be. He already loved someone.

Paige went to bed that night feeling sad, lonely, and guilty.

She took her computer with her to her room, setting it up next to the bed, the way she often did when she slept, just in case any ideas for her thesis came to her in the night.

She settled back with her eyes closed, waiting for sleep to claim her.

It didn't take long for her to realize that she couldn't sleep. Not now. Not when closing her eyes just brought back images of the crime scene instead. Not when her mind was still in turmoil over everything that had almost, but not quite, happened with Christopher.

Because she couldn't sleep, Paige picked up the computer and pulled up the files on Adam Riker. She'd been over her transcripts and her notes many times before, but she was hoping that she'd missed something in it all: something that would lead her to Adam. She had to do something about this. She couldn't just let Adam keep killing. She wasn't a detective, but maybe, just maybe, she could make up for some of the mistakes she'd made by working out where he was going to go next.

Paige hunted back through the files, reading them carefully, not daring to skim any of them now in case the detail she needed was hidden in the rest of the text. This wasn't the moment for word searches to try to narrow things down, or for hunting after things she'd half remembered, like the existence of Adam's uncle; this was the moment for doing things properly, for reading every sentence, every word. She couldn't afford to miss anything.

To give her another way of trying to find an answer, Paige turned on the audio files for her thesis, taken from the sessions. Adam's voice came through loud and clear, sending a shiver down Paige's spine while she lay there. It was hard not to imagine him there in the room with her.

"You want to know why I do this, Paige? Isn't that rather a boring question?"

"My thesis is about why people who commit crimes like this choose to do what they do. I thought it would be interesting to try and actually answer the question."

"Oh no, there's nothing interesting about it. But then, people like you are boring. You sit there, you take notes, and you don't think about how you could be helping anyone."

"I'm not the one who's committing these crimes."

"No, I am. But you know, I think there's a way that you can help me, Paige. I think you could tell me about yourself. What's your favorite color?"

Paige remembered the conversation as the recorded words washed over her. At the time, she'd thought that the question didn't mean anything, and if it helped to build rapport, then maybe it was a good way to start to get more out of Adam.

"Teal."

"A mixed color. A fashionable color. Are you someone who can't make up her mind, Paige? Or are you someone who tries to keep up with fashion?"

"Maybe I just like teal."

Now, Paige found herself wondering which of her answers had been one answer too far. Which one had given Adam enough to look up every detail of her life. Maybe, if one of the guards had been helping him even then, Paige had gone too far the moment she'd set foot in that room with him for their sessions.

"Now you have to tell me something in return," Paige's voice said, on the recording.

"Have to?"

Paige could imagine Adam shaking his head at that.

"I don't *have* to do anything, Paige. I don't even have to talk to you."

"Then why do you choose to?"

"Because there's something about you that intrigues me. You seem… special, but you have drawbacks."

"Such as?" Paige asked.

"Your inability to see things the way they really are, for one."

"I'm sorry?"

"Not only can you not see the truth; you can't accept it, either."

"I'm sorry, you're going to have to explain that one to me."

"It's just the way you are, Paige. You don't want to know the truth because you don't want to know how wrong you really are on this. I think that's why you want to do that thesis, actually. You've convinced yourself that there's some great meaning behind all of this, and you want to prove that to yourself. You want to prove that you were right about something. But you know what? You're wrong. There is no greater meaning to any of it. That idea was all just a dream. A fantasy that you've been living in for far too long."

Paige remembered how she'd felt at those words, how she'd been hurt by them.

"When you write your thesis, I think it's probably going to be a very boring one. You know, most people would say that the truth is a lot more interesting than any dream."

"But not you."

"The truth is boring. It's nothing like you think it is. I think everyone wants to believe that the truth is complicated; but actually, it's simple."

"And what's the truth, then?" Paige asked, on the recording.

A pause, as Adam considered his answer.

"The truth is that in the end, you're all alone. That no one can ever understand you. That no one can ever truly love you, because they don't know you. They aren't *like* you. I don't need to ask if you understand that, Paige. I know."

Perhaps he had known. Perhaps he'd known all about Paige's life, even then.

"Tell me, Paige, do you ever go home, to your family?"

Looking back with hindsight, it was obvious then that he'd known all about Paige. She just hadn't seen it at the time, cocooned in an illusion of safety that came from Adam being locked away, supposedly for good. It had been a game where they'd both been playing, but only he had known that.

"That's not something I'd like to talk about," Paige's voice said on the recording.

"No?" Adam said. "I completely understand. Family is another trap. Another thing that people tell you is important. Would you like to hear about my family home, out in the sticks? About the place where my father used to try to beat the evil out of me whenever I did anything he didn't like? As a kid, I used to want to burn it down, preferably with my father inside, but fire has never been my... medium of choice."

Paige remembered that she'd thought that it was a joke, a bad joke. She'd never believed that Adam had really wanted to talk about his family home like that.

Lying there alone in the dark, Paige remembered how she'd shaken her head, and Adam had nodded in response.

"It's alright. That's another thing that I know that you know. That's another reason why we get along. Why I'm prepared to talk to you. You understand me in a way that no one else can. And I understand you. You know that I'm like you, in many ways. You know that I'm the same as you, in many ways. Even if you don't want to admit it. Even if you don't want to admit that there's any truth in what I'm saying."

Paige had thought that Adam was just trying to get under her skin, but now she wasn't so sure. She thought now that it might be something both deeper and more dangerous than that.

"Now that you're an adult, do you still want to burn it down?" Paige had asked. She could remember Adam giving a small snort of laughter.

"My father is dead. I killed him. My mother is gone. Burning it all would not exorcise any ghosts, and I wouldn't do something like that for the enjoyment. But perhaps... I would quite like to stand there and see it again as a man, not a child. What is the trite modern term? I would like... a sense of closure."

Listening to the recordings, Paige stopped short. She thought she knew then where Adam might go. His family home had been looked into in the initial investigation into his crimes, but now didn't belong to him. For that reason, she imagined that Christopher wouldn't give it much attention.

But the first two killings had the sense of completing unfinished business about them to Paige. If Adam really had wanted to see his family home again for the closure, well, wasn't there every chance that he might go there now?

CHAPTER SEVENTEEN

Paige wasn't entirely surprised when Christopher wanted to drive straight out to the house the next morning. He'd been quick to jump on the leads she gave him before, which left Paige wondering if she was the only source of leads that he had when it came to Adam Riker.

There was a kind of responsibility that came with that, the weight of which seemed to settle onto Paige's shoulders as they drove together.

In spite of everything Christopher had said to try to reassure her before, it made all of this her responsibility. If she didn't provide him with the right leads, then there was a chance that Adam could get away. That she'd let a criminal slip through her fingers. That he would keep killing, and no one would stop him.

It just wasn't something she could afford to allow herself to think.

"So you're telling me that you think he might go there?" Christopher asked as they were driving out, taking roads out into the countryside.

"He told me about the house. He said that he wanted to see it again. That he wanted closure. And the killings so far seem to have been about tying up loose ends from the past."

"That makes a kind of sense. The house is where he said his father abused him?"

"'Trying to beat the evil out of him,' he said," Paige echoed Adam's words as closely as she could. She'd learned with Adam that the details mattered.

Christopher nodded, and there was an uncomfortable silence in the moments that followed.

"Then it seems like a good place to try."

Paige had imagined that she'd be nervous about going somewhere that Adam was likely to be, just as she had been back at the farmhouse. In truth, she wasn't. The only thing she felt was a kind of determination that she wasn't going to let Adam get away with anything. She couldn't help but feel like the answers were all within reach. All she had to do was take them, like reaching out to pick an apple from a tree. Yet somehow, she hadn't managed it so far. She couldn't quite find the right parts of her notes to lead them straight to Adam.

Currently, her notes were leading her and Christopher out into the countryside, down back lanes barely wide enough for Christopher's car. When a pickup truck came the other way, they had to pull almost all the way into a hedge to avoid it. Based on the things Adam had said, Paige found herself imagining the place where he had lived as some run-down shack in the middle of nowhere.

The place they found was nothing like that. In fact, it was a large, well-kept house. The paintwork was still in good condition, the garden was neat and trim. Paige couldn't find a single thing that indicated that this was the house that Adam had been talking about. It could have belonged to anyone.

"This isn't right," Paige said. "We're not in the right place."

"This was the only thing you had to go on. It's not your fault," Christopher said.

"I know, but... look at it. It's *clearly* not the family home of a sadistic murderer."

"What does one of those look like?" Christopher countered.

Paige still wanted to know what was going on. This didn't seem anything like the kind of place Adam had described when talking about his childhood. "Maybe we should walk up and check that we're in the right place?"

Christopher nodded, drawing the car to a halt in front of the house. Even as he did so, the front door opened, revealing a man and a woman standing there, with a couple of kids running around their legs as they struggled to be the first to see what was going on.

"This can't be right," Paige said again. This was all far too bright and happy to have anything to do with the life of Adam Riker.

"It's the address that's on the file for his former family home," Christopher insisted.

The two of them got out and approached. Christopher did the talking.

"I'm Agent Marriott, with the FBI," he said, showing his ID. "Is this Grove View?"

Out this far in the country, the name of the house seemed to mean more than the address, and Paige guessed that even the GPS might be wrong.

"That's right," the man said, with a slight frown. "Did you say the FBI? What's this about?"

That caught Paige a little by surprise, but she took a guess anyway. "When did you buy this house, sir?"

102

"About three years back," he said. "We've been renovating it ever since."

Which put it right around the time Adam had finally found himself put away for good.

They were in the right place. It had just changed beyond recognition in the meantime. Paige could only imagine how Adam would react to that. Would he be disappointed? Or would he see it as confirmation of his hatred? Would he take one look at it and walk away?

Paige's guess was that he would be angry, and she didn't want to think about what an angry serial killer might do to anyone there in the house when he showed up.

"And were you told anything about the house's history when you bought it?" Christopher asked, sounding just as worried as Paige felt right then.

Looks of concern came over the couple's faces then. "What is it? There aren't bodies buried under it, or something?"

Paige wished that she could say no, but with Adam, it was impossible to be sure. Only no, there couldn't be, not that anyone knew about. If any murders had actually occurred in the house, the realtor would have had to declare that. They *didn't* have to declare the connection to a serial killer though.

"Was there anything you were told about the previous owners that made you think twice about the purchase?"

"Nothing," the woman said. "It was a good price. There was some work that needed to be done after we moved in, but we didn't mind that."

"What about the neighbors?" Paige asked. "Have you spoken to them about this place?"

"It's a quiet area," the man said. "Our nearest neighbors are at least a mile away. Most of the other people around here are older. I think some of them have been here for years. Seriously, what's all this about?"

Christopher gave the children around the couple's feet a pointed look, obviously not wanting to talk about Adam in front of them. The woman seemed to get the message, ushering them inside.

"Ok, kids, that's enough looking at the strangers. Go and play in your room. We need to talk to them."

"Mom!"

"Now, please."

They complained, but at least they went, hurrying back inside the house. It left Paige and Christopher free to talk about the difficult part of all this: what had happened here, and just who might be coming.

"This house used to belong to the family of a man named Adam Riker," Christopher said.

Paige saw the shift in the expressions of the couple there at the door as they started to understand what was going on. They knew exactly who Adam was. They must have seen the news reports, seen the crime scenes. Adam Riker was infamous.

"Oh my God," the wife said. "And you're here because... oh my God... is he coming here? I mean, do you think he's coming here?"

"It's possible. We can't be sure, I don't want to worry you, but it's possible," Christopher said.

"Why would he come here?" the man said. "What would he want with us?"

Paige shook her head. "It's not about you, personally. It's about this place. It's about him wanting to return to the place where he grew up now that he's free again. It's about him wanting to find some kind of closure."

"A serial killer wants closure?" the man said. "But we don't know him. We just bought this place."

"It won't matter that he doesn't know you. What matters is that he's trying to return home, and this isn't his home anymore. When he gets here... he won't be happy that it has changed."

She was certain of that much from her sessions. Adam didn't react well to things not being the way he expected them to be. He liked being the one in control of things.

"So what are you saying?" the woman asked.

"You might be in danger if you stay here," Christopher said.

That was put more bluntly than Paige would have said it, but that didn't make it any less true. Adam was a dangerous man, and there was no telling what he might do.

"Are you saying that we should go?" the man asked.

"Your safety is our top priority. But if you had somewhere else that you could go for a few days, it would be for the best," Christopher said.

Paige saw the man bristle slightly at that suggestion.

"You think we should just up and run because of the possibility that some escaped prisoner might be coming here? You think I can't protect my own family?"

104

Paige could understand that feeling of protectiveness, and that ego driven desire not to back down from any danger, but she also knew just how dangerous it could be, for both this man and his family. He didn't know what was coming, not really. Unlike Paige, he hadn't sat down opposite Adam, and seen that dead expression staring back.

So she said the only thing she could think of to cut through it all. She hated having to do it, but she knew right then that it was the only way to keep these people safe.

"No, I don't think you can. Not against Adam. If he comes here, you won't see him coming. You won't be able to protect anyone. Who is in the house?"

"Me, my wife, our younger son and daughter, and our older daughter."

Paige hated what she had to say next, but she knew that if she didn't, these people would insist on staying here, and that would put them at risk. She had to be harsh about this, because it was the only way to save their lives.

"He'll kill you first," Paige said to the man. "He'll probably do it quickly. Most likely, you won't even see it coming. Adam has taken men as victims before, but given the choice, he seems to prefer women. He'll kill your younger children quickly, too. Your wife and your eldest daughter, though... he likes to tie his victims up, and torture them, until finally their bodies can't take the strain of it anymore."

"Paige, that's enough," Christopher said. "That isn't... you can't do that."

It was done, though, and Paige was sure that she'd had the effect she needed to. Paige saw the man swallow, his fear obvious. Even though that was the point of everything Paige had just said, she hated that she'd had to say it.

"You want to protect your family," Christopher said, in a much more conciliatory tone. "But the best way you can do that right now is to take them to a motel for a couple of days, or to visit relatives somewhere. *That's* how you keep them safe."

"What about our house?" the woman said, obviously not liking the idea of leaving it empty while Adam came to look around.

"We'll take care of it. We'll make sure that he doesn't do any damage. Just go," Christopher said.

Paige watched as the couple looked at one another, then nodded. They headed back into the house, the man calling out.

"Kids! I need you to pack a bag. We're going to visit Aunt Rene for a couple of days!"

He was obviously trying to make it sound like an exciting adventure, but Paige could hear the note of fear in his voice. While they started to make preparations, Paige turned to Christopher.

"I hate having to scare people like that."

Christopher nodded. "It's hard to play the bad guy, but if it keeps them safe, it's worth it."

And now they were going to be there instead.

"If we're here, that's going to mean he's coming after us, isn't it?" she said.

"Yes. But it's better than the alternative. You don't have to be here, though, Paige."

"I want to be," Paige replied, instantly.

"I'm serious."

"So am I," she shot back. "If you have to take me back, he could come while you're doing it. And what if I'm wrong again? What if I go home, and he comes for me?"

She didn't want to be home alone. Not tonight.

"All right," Christopher said with a sigh. "Looks like we're waiting here together. Adam will come, and we'll be waiting for him."

CHAPTER EIGHTEEN

Staking out Adam's old home meant waiting. Waiting, and watching, with Paige hoping that she was right this time.

The day wore on with Paige and Christopher in Adam Riker's old house. Paige found herself walking through it, hoping that it would give her some improved sense of who Adam was. She wasn't getting much. She'd been back to her notes several times, looking through the interviews, trying to find other possibilities, but he'd mentioned this place several times. It meant something to him.

The renovations meant that the house wasn't the same one it would have been when Adam was a child. She tried to imagine it as it might have been then, but it was hard. The house they were in was clean and modern, and that meant that it was hard for Paige to make the leap to how Adam's home had once looked.

Paige wasn't sure what she'd been expecting. Part of her had always thought that coming to the house would give her a sense of Adam. She'd thought that maybe she'd be able to feel him there in the lines of the place, but the truth was that she felt nothing.

"It's really just us?" she asked, as Christopher paced the place, obviously anxious as he waited for the possibility of Adam arriving. "No vans of agents sitting outside?"

"After the last time, I don't think I can swing another full stakeout," Christopher said.

Paige knew that was her fault. They'd only spent last night staking out George Riker's address because Paige had been so certain that Adam would show up there. They'd all wasted their time, and Adam had been in Sara Langdon's office instead, murdering her.

If they couldn't get backup now, it was because she was the one who'd cried wolf, however much she'd thought she was right at the time. She just hoped that she was right this time. It was why she kept going back to her notes, checking other possibilities. As far as Paige could see, though, this was the last major link to Adam's past left, now that they had his uncle watched and Adam had killed two women that he had a history with.

107

"It's not your fault," Christopher said, obviously guessing that Paige was thinking about it again. "You gave it your best shot; you just happened to guess wrong."

Paige wished that she could think of it as something to be put aside that easily, rather than as yet another failure.

She went to sit on the front porch, trying to ignore the smell of fresh paint. She could have done more. She could have expected more. She could have been better.

Paige was sure that Christopher had told her that it wasn't her fault again, but she had missed it. She was too busy staring out of the window waiting for Adam.

"I wasn't thinking straight," she said. "George Riker felt like the obvious choice, and I just... I should have been more careful."

"Well, that's the risk we take," Christopher said. "Look, you need to focus on something else for a while."

"Like what?" Paige asked. It wasn't as if there was a lot to do other than think while they waited.

"Well, there's the possibility that a dangerous psychopath might be coming through the door later. Do you know how to shoot?"

That question caught Paige by surprise. She shook her head.

"Seriously?" Christopher asked.

"I've never needed to," she said. It wasn't something she'd ever had any interest in.

"Well, let's rectify that. We might be facing off against a killer. I'm not going to have you in the middle of that without being able to protect yourself."

"Now?" Paige asked. "What about if Adam shows up?"

"Then we deal with him," Christopher said. "It's something you need to know, and there's no time like the present."

Paige didn't think that was such a good idea, but she followed the FBI agent as he led the way to the kitchen, grabbing a couple of bottles of beer from the refrigerator. Since they were stuck there without obvious supplies, Paige guessed that it made a kind of sense to use what was there. No doubt the FBI would pay the family back later.

After that, Paige followed Christopher as he went out to his car. He got out a box of bullets, drew his service weapon, and then led her out into the yard beyond the house.

He set up the bottles on a tree stump at one end of the garden, leaving Paige at the other. He walked back to her and handed her the gun, carefully.

"Okay, this is a berretta, 9mm. I want you to hold it as you might do to shoot something. The safety is currently on, see it here."

Paige did as Christopher instructed, then he took the gun back.

"Keep your finger clear of the trigger till you're ready to shoot."

He showed her how to hold the gun, how to line up the sights on the target and how to pull the trigger.

"Okay, we're going to go through the gun safety rules and then I'm going to let you shoot. Got it?"

"Yes."

"The safety is off, the finger is off the trigger and you're ready to fire. Always assume that the gun is loaded, and never point it at anything you don't want to shoot."

Paige nodded.

"Good. Okay, your finger is on the trigger, and you know how to fire. Lean into the shot, so that the recoil doesn't send it off target."

"Like this?" Paige asked.

"Not quite." Christopher was close to her then, adjusting her position. He was professional and efficient, but Paige was all too aware of him standing close behind her. Close enough that the adjustments might have felt like... more, if Paige didn't know already that Christopher had a wife. "Start with the weapon close to your chest, then move out into a solid firing position. If you actually have to use a gun, my guess is that it will take place at close range. I want you to aim for the bottles, and then, when you're ready, pull the trigger."

It was impossible not to think about how close to her Christopher was then. Paige had to push those thoughts away, reminding herself that he was a married man. She didn't even think that he was aware of that closeness in the same way. She forced herself to focus on aiming instead. She fired the gun, a sharp recoil immediately pushing her back slightly, the sound of the shot ringing in her ears.

She watched as a bullet hit the target, shattering one of the bottles, sending shards of glass flying into the air.

"Good!" Christopher said. "You're a natural at this."

Paige was surprised by how easy it felt, and how good, although she suspected that had something to do with the presence of Christopher there so close to her. She didn't feel any joy at the destruction, but there *was* a kind of satisfaction at being able to do this properly.

"Again," Christopher said.

Paige aimed at the other bottle, focusing in on it and bracing herself as she fired again. Once more, the bottle smashed into fragments as the bullet hit it. Again, there was that surge of happiness that came with succeeding, even if it was at something destructive.

At the very least, it meant that if Adam showed up, Paige would be ready for him.

*

Day was wearing into night, little by little. Paige kept going through her notes on her sessions with Adam, revising them the way she might have for an exam, trying to cram in as much information about him as possible.

It would have been impossible to relax, if Christopher hadn't been there in the house with her. Even with him there, Paige worried about everything that might happen, and everything that had happened so far. She kept going over it in her head, what she'd said to Adam, what she'd done, what she might have done differently.

Christopher had told her to focus on something else, and she had, but it was impossible not to think about Adam, about how she had been fooled by him. He'd known everything about her.

Christopher was making food, using the contents of the kitchen, since it was too far out of the city to just call for takeout.

"You cook a lot?" Paige asked.

"When I'm home, I like to cook for Justine and myself," Christopher said. "It's nice to do normal things when so much of my job isn't normal."

"What does your wife think of your job?"

It was strange, talking with this man she felt a thread of attraction towards about his wife, but maybe it was what Paige needed. She had to remind herself that Christopher wasn't available, that he hadn't shown any signs of reciprocating the things that Paige found herself starting to feel towards him.

"She doesn't like that it puts me in danger," Christopher said. "Or that it often keeps me away from home. Chasing the worst kinds of criminals isn't a nine to five job."

Paige wanted to know more about his life, more about him. She couldn't settle, though. She knew that it was just nerves. Adam was approaching. It was all she could think about.

110

"Beef ramen with a miso broth," Christopher said, setting a plate of handmade noodles down in front of her.

Paige had to admit that it was good, eating there at the kitchen table with Christopher. There was something almost intimate about it, and Paige had to remind herself that this wasn't some kind of romantic dinner. This was a stakeout, waiting for a serial killer. This was work. His work, at least.

They were halfway through the meal when Paige heard a sound, a creak deeper in the house. It took her a moment or two to realize that it was the sound of a window creaking open.

Someone was trying to get into the house, and Paige could only think of one person that might be.

"Adam is here," Christopher said, getting to his feet and drawing his berretta.

Paige stood up, following him, the two of them standing in the kitchen, waiting, hoping that they were right, while they listened to the sound of movement upstairs. Paige heard the creak of the stairs, and Christopher started forward, his gun ready in his hands.

In spite of the training that she'd had earlier, Paige was glad that it was Christopher with the weapon, not her. Being able to shoot a couple of bottles wasn't the same thing as taking on a serial killer in the dark.

They moved through the house together, heading for the stairs, Paige following close behind Christopher. It was probably dangerous to be heading *towards* a serial killer, but it felt more dangerous to wait alone in the dark in a house that might have Adam in it.

It was dark in most of the house now, but Christopher didn't turn on the lights. He used a flashlight instead, presumably so that the beam against the darkness might blind anyone he pointed it at.

As they reached the stairs, Paige thought that she saw a flicker of movement there above.

"There!" she shouted, pointing.

Instantly, Christopher had his weapon and his flashlight pointed.

"Freeze! FBI! Don't move!"

The figure there froze, hands going in the air instantly as Christopher's flashlight played over him. Paige found a light switch and flicked it on.

The sudden wash of light revealed, not Adam, but a teenage boy, dressed in a dark hoodie and jeans, with spiked hair and a ring through his nose. Even the fear he showed was the very opposite of anything Adam might have displayed.

111

"Don't shoot!" he said. "I'm sorry! I... I'm just here to see Celeste."

"Who's Celeste?" Christopher demanded, in a stern tone.

Paige could guess, though, just based on the age of the boy. "The eldest daughter. We've caught a kid sneaking in to make out."

It was a false alarm, but that didn't mean that Adam wasn't coming. The kid had just shown how easy it was for someone to get into the house. That meant that they still had to wait, and watch, and be ready if he did show up.

CHAPTER NINETEEN

Adam waited and watched in the dark, barely moving as he stared out, trying to pick his moment. He had all night, if he needed it. He could see lights on in the house ahead of him, letting him watch the figure of a woman through the window, letting him trace every step she took, every movement she made. She moved between the kitchen and the front room, with Adam's eyes tracking her all the way.

He was patient, waiting out of sight, letting the darkness hide him. He would act once it was time to act, and not a moment before. He would wait all night if he had to. He would leave his hiding place among a couple of trees only once he was sure that he was safe to move forward.

If being caught once had taught him anything, and it had, then it was to be cautious even when he'd planned out every step of what he was going to do. He'd seen firsthand how easily unexpected factors could throw off even his most carefully considered efforts, so now he was working to make sure that none would interfere.

The woman was eating now, some kind of takeout, probably Chinese, judging by the cartons set on the counter. Adam waited for her to eat, still watching, still trying to find the perfect moment. Adam had been almost ready to move when the delivery driver had arrived, but now he was back to waiting and watching. He wasn't going to let there be any interruptions. They both had time, he and his prey.

He wondered where Paige was now. Was she in bed, or at home eating takeout of her own? Was she sitting there, working on her thesis?

It was more likely, Adam suspected, that she was out chasing after another lead that she thought might find him. Adam didn't know whether to be pleased or annoyed that she was putting so much effort into trying to find him. It was almost flattering in a way that she would give him her full attention; it made her feel all the more special to him, but at the same time, Adam had no love for being hunted.

Still, it was all a part of his plan. All a part of the steps they both needed to go through.

113

He'd seen her on the news, arriving at the places he'd been, just a step behind. He'd been pleased for her as she did so, knowing that Paige would be one of the few people in a position to truly appreciate the depths of his art. After all she'd been through, Adam knew that she had to understand.

He'd seen the FBI agent she'd been with, too. Adam had felt something else then, a flash of something surprisingly close to jealousy at the sight of Paige there with someone who wasn't him. He'd seen how close she'd looked to the man who'd escorted her into the crime scenes, and that... irritated Adam more than he had imagined that it might. Strange.

Adam had to remind himself that if she was going to follow him and try to find him, then of course she would find herself working with someone. Of course she would find herself partnered with someone from the FBI. It wasn't something that Paige could do alone, however much Adam might wish her to. The FBI weren't just going to let a psychologist wander around after him on her own, and after the things he'd said back at the institution, he was sure that they *all* thought he was coming for Paige.

He wondered how long it would be before Paige realized that he'd chosen everything he said in their sessions very carefully. Perhaps she had already but was still insisting on following the breadcrumbs he'd laid down. Adam remembered every session, every word that he and Paige had said. Of course he could remember, given the special connection that existed between the two of them. Adam had felt that connection every time they were together in their sessions. He had dreamed about her sometimes at night. In about half of those dreams, he'd been killing her, stringing her up as helplessly as any of his other victims. In the other half, they'd been sitting there together somewhere on a beach or in a cabin, happy together, content in a way that Adam was never truly content.

That contentment never lasted past the dawn. Adam certainly wasn't content now. Instead, he felt the need to act, to kill. That restlessness sat deep inside of him, refusing to go away.

Maybe killing the woman in front of him would be one step closer to that contentment. Adam wondered if she thought about everything that she'd done. Every wrong that she had committed, the wound that she had inflicted that had brought them to this point. He would have to ask her, although since the house had close neighbors, he might have to

114

gag her before he got many answers. Certainly, once he started his work.

First, though, Adam had to find a way in that wouldn't raise the alarm. Because of the neighbors close by, because one of them had a dog, and because of how much this woman moved around the house, it wouldn't be safe to do what he usually did and creep forward to pick a lock. The locks on his target's door were solid enough that they would take a minute or two of his time, and there was too much of a chance to be spotted.

That left two approaches. Option one was to wait until the dead of night before he acted, when she was likely to be asleep, and so were her neighbors. If it came to it, Adam would do that, but right now he itched with the need to do something, to feel the kind of satisfaction that could only come from killing someone. Waiting would be a kind of slow torture for him, although he supposed that was only fair. That was why he was keeping such a close eye on the building, trying to find something that would work as option two.

While he waited, Adam considered what he knew of the woman within. He made it his business to know. Angelique Philips, twenty-three, worked as a web administrator for a company here in D.C. Went on vacation to Thailand and Goa when she could afford it. Pretty, of course, given what she'd done, with long blonde hair and the kind of figure that made men stare. One look at her social media had shown Adam that she knew it. Vanity, all was vanity.

This wasn't about her vanity, though. This was about what she'd done. This was about making things right.

Adam saw a potential opportunity when he saw her cat: some huge fluffy Maine Coon, which clearly wanted to go outside, and Adam couldn't see a cat flap. Adam crept forward. He would be in view for a brief time, but he believed that it was worth the risk. Even if he were spotted, he could leave and come back in the night, without it being a problem.

It was worth taking a chance to do this for Paige.

He timed his approach beautifully, carrying his bag of ropes with him, reaching the door just as it started to swing open to let the cat out. The creature ran past Adam, and he ignored it as he wrenched the door wide open, so that Angelique was looking him square in the face, a look of stunned shock on her features.

Adam spun her and had a drug-soaked cloth over her mouth before she could cry out, dragging her back into the house. Angelique seemed to come back to herself as Adam did that, trying to claw at his eyes, but Adam kept his head tucked, ignoring her attempts. Slowly, her struggles started to weaken. Finally, she went limp, and Adam let her slump to the floor, unconscious, but not yet dead. Adam was careful about that part.

Good. They could get started.

He dragged Angelique through to her living room, moving her almost gently, shutting the back door to her house behind him. The living room was an elegant picture of grays and greens, the kind of thing that an interior designer might have picked out, without any real hint of her personality. There were no personal pictures, just prints that looked as if they might hang on walls across the country, while the furniture was modern and bland.

Adam got out his ropes, trying to consider the aesthetics of what he was doing. He had at least as much taste in some matters as Angelique's interior designer. He guessed that Paige would see the resulting tableaux, so Adam wanted to make it as perfect as he could.

He started to tie Angelique, twisting her, contorting her so that her body was bent back impossibly. As much as he would have liked to hear her attempts to justify herself, Adam couldn't risk her neighbors hearing her scream for help, so he gagged her instead.

Somewhere in it all, she woke, starting to struggle. Not that it made any difference at this point.

Adam took a seat opposite her, in one of those oh so modern chairs that she'd chosen to furnish her house with, observing her carefully. It was far from comfortable, but compared to Angelique's current position, he suspected it wasn't so bad.

"Hello, Angelique," he said, in a cold tone. "Do you know who I am? Have you been watching the news?"

Her attempt to scream and fight free suggested that she had been watching, and that she knew perfectly well who Adam was. That was good. He wanted her to be afraid. She deserved it. He wanted her to feel every moment of pain and fear that he could bring her.

Adam took out a knife and set it down on a glass surfaced table. He watched as her eyes tracked the metal gleam of it frantically.

"Do you know why I'm doing this, Angelique?"

She shook her head, or tried to. Given how tightly tied she was, there wasn't a lot of scope for her to move even that much.

"I'm doing this because of what *you* did."

116

Adam saw that she was crying now. Did she think that would have any effect on him? Did she think that it made any kind of difference to what was going to happen to her? Did she think that he was that weak?

"Do you remember what you did, Angelique? Do you remember what you did to Paige?"

Angelique started to shake her head, and Adam struck her then, in a stinging, open handed blow.

"Liar! Do you think I don't know when people lie? Do you think I let them get away with trying to deceive me?"

More tears then, streaming down her face, in some mix of fear, pain and more general distress. It was almost as bad as lying, as far as Adam was concerned. When he'd been a boy, he hadn't been allowed tears. Those had just earned him a worse beating. He'd quickly learned not to cry.

"You betrayed Paige," Adam said. "You hurt her, wounded her. You claimed to be her friend, but you seduced the young man she was in love with. You helped to break her heart. You stole him away. You hurt her, just because you could. Those aren't the actions of a friend, Angelique. Those are the actions of an enemy. Someone trying to destroy her."

Adam stood so sharply that Angelique tried to reel back, but that just meant more pain for her, as Adam had known it would. He'd become quite expert at what he did. At judging the effects of everything he did on other people.

"Tell me, Angelique, are you finding it difficult to breathe yet? Are you feeling the pressure in your head starting to rise as the blood flows there? Are you starting to feel that you can't hold this position?"

Adam stood just a pace or two away from her, smiling at her as his words made her struggle.

"If not, you will feel it. It's such a slow death, fighting against it every step of the way. Some people last hours before they die. You won't. You don't have the strength for it. You aren't anything like Paige. *She* has strength."

She was trying to talk through her gag now. Adam had no interest in hearing anything that she had to say.

"So pretty," he said. "But that prettiness is what you used to hurt Paige, and I can't allow that. You have to *pay* for that."

He picked up the knife.

"Paige and I have such a special connection. She'll see it, in time. She'll see that her proper place is beside me, not chasing me. Of

117

course, you'll be dead by then. Now, should I cut you, do you think? Should I carve up that pretty flesh so that no man would ever want you, even if you weren't dead?"

That had a certain kind of potential as an idea, but Adam was very aware that Paige would be coming to this place soon enough. He wanted Angelique recognizable. Besides, cutting her would only hasten her death.

For what she'd done to Paige, Adam found that he wanted her to suffer.

So he sat back in the chair instead, watching, unblinking and unmoving. Angelique breathed a sigh of relief, but that was only because she didn't understand how bad things were going to get, given time.

"I'm going to sit here and watch you," Adam said, holding the knife carefully. "I'm going to watch while your body slowly kills itself, because it can't move well enough to let you breathe. I'm going to watch and know that you can't do anything about it. Most importantly though, I'm going to watch, and know that you deserve every, single, moment of this."

Angelique struggled against her bonds again, then. Adam just sat back and watched her with ferocious intensity. He had all night.

CHAPTER TWENTY

Paige was walking through Adam's childhood home, trying to make some sense of his life. In spite of the changes that the renovations had wrought, Paige was starting to feel that she could practically see him in front of her as a child, see the beatings that had helped to shape him. His father was there, a vague figure, conjured only by Adam's descriptions so that he was halfway to being a demonic presence in Paige's mind's eye.

The house might have been renovated, but there were still parts of it that looked as if they might have come from deep in the past. There were whole sections now with peeling plasterwork and creaking floorboards, lending an ominous atmosphere to it all as Paige made her way through it, step by step.

Come to think of it, had it been this large when Paige had checked it over with Christopher earlier? She felt almost sure that it hadn't. Paige felt as though she'd gotten turned around in it somehow, because she now seemed to be lost within the expanse of the place. There seemed to be twists and turns to it in the dark that were making it hard for Paige to find her way. She couldn't even seem to find a light switch that would let her see where she was going.

Paige felt her way through the house instead, trying to get a sense of where she was by touch as much as by the shadows that seemed to mask everything.

"Christopher? Christopher, are you there?"

There wasn't any answer, and Paige found the sense of unease running through her starting to intensify. She was sure as she tried to make her way back that something was wrong. Badly wrong.

Christopher was meant to be here. He was meant to be with her, looking out for her. They were both meant to be in Adam Riker's childhood home, waiting for him to arrive, trying to catch him. So where was Christopher? Had something happened to him?

Was Paige suddenly alone here? That was a terrifying thought. What if Adam came now? Paige had started to have doubts about whether he was going to show up right around the time when the boy had sneaked in. Now, though, Paige felt certain that Adam was going to show up.

She was alone in this house, and Adam was coming, and there was no way that it was just to see his old house; he was coming for her. Paige was certain of it.

"Christopher?" she called out again.

She needed to get back to him. She needed to be close to him, and not just because it felt like the safest place to be right then. Paige had wanted to get closer to him, wanted him to hold her close and tell her that everything was all right. She knew that he had a wife, but Paige was a psychologist; she knew as well as anyone that just knowing that a thing was wrong didn't stop someone from wanting it. All it affected was whether they would act on that feeling.

Paige had more self-control than that, but it didn't affect the fact that right then, she wanted to be near Christopher. This house was *far* too creepy.

Paige was still making her way back through it when she heard the creak of a floorboard somewhere behind her. She wanted to tell herself that this was just one more kid breaking in, but somehow, she knew that it wasn't.

Paige turned slowly, trying to find out what was going on, hoping that it would be Christopher, even as she knew that it wasn't. She spun to face the sound, and there, standing in the middle of the hallway Paige was in, was Adam.

He stared at her levelly, with the kind of coldness to his expression that Paige remembered from their last session, when he'd thrown facts about her life at her like they were sharp splinters of glass. There was an awful intensity to that expression. He started to advance on Paige, and she found herself backing away without even meaning to.

"What's wrong, Paige?" he asked. "You've been trying to find me, haven't you? Well, here I am. You found me. Aren't you happy that you found me?"

"Christopher!" Paige cried out, calling for help as loud as she could. "Help!"

"He isn't coming," Adam said. "He can't save you now."

What did that mean? Had Adam already done something to hurt Christopher? Had he killed him? Had he murdered Christopher so that he wouldn't be in the way when Adam came for Paige? That thought brought a note of panic to her, both because of what might have happened to Christopher, and because of what it implied about what Adam was going to do next.

He'd gotten Christopher out of the way, which implied that he wanted to take his time with Paige. Even as Paige thought it, Adam stretched a length of rope between his hands, the threat to Paige obvious.

Paige knew in an instant that she needed to get out of there. She had to find a way to escape. She couldn't imagine being able to fight Adam like that. She turned and ran instead, sprinting away from him, not caring that she didn't know her way through the house in the dark. Paige tripped over something, got to her feet, and ran again.

She didn't dare look back, because in the dark that just seemed like a recipe for falling over again, and this time, it seemed to Paige that she might not have enough time to get up. She turned left, and inexplicably found herself heading up a flight of stairs.

Adam was close behind her, the tread of his feet on the stairs coming a fraction after Paige's. He grabbed for her then, and Paige tried to fight free, but Adam's weight slammed into her, sending her crashing down onto the stairs, the impact knocking the breath out of her. Adam was on top of her then, holding her down in spite of Paige's efforts to get free.

Paige felt the ropes starting to wrap round her then, wrenching her arms behind her back. She saw the flash of a knife then, with Adam standing over her, and in that moment, Paige knew that she was going to die.

Paige woke gasping, with someone standing over her, the figure indistinct. She lashed out automatically, and he jumped back, evading her attack with ease.

"Paige, it's me," Christopher said, holding up his hands to show that he was no threat. "It's me. You were sleeping and crying out."

Paige took several panting breaths as she realized what had just happened. She'd been asleep. It was just a dream. It was a dream, and Adam hadn't actually been there. She was safe, however much her heart was telling her otherwise right then, beating far faster than she would have liked.

Paige slowly realized that she was sitting in a chair in the living room of Adam's childhood home and daylight was streaming in through the window. She realized a moment or two later that she must have fallen asleep, and instantly felt guilty, because she was meant to be there keeping watch for Adam.

"Were you awake all night?" Paige asked Christopher.

"I had to make sure that he wouldn't show up," he said.

And he clearly hadn't. Paige realized that not only had she fallen asleep, but she'd guessed wrong, yet again. She'd put Christopher in a position where he'd had to stand watch all night, because he'd relied on her, and she'd messed up once more.

"I keep guessing wrong," Paige said. "I was so sure that he would come here."

"He still might," Christopher replied. "But I don't think we can spend any more time waiting here. Every minute we spend here is a minute he could be using to get further away. I'll see if I can call in anyone to watch the house, but-"

His phone rang in that moment, and Christopher answered instantly.

"Marriott. What's happening?"

The way his expression changed gave Paige a clue to the answer to that. His face went grave, his eyes narrowing as he listened.

"Yes, I understand. What's the address? Yes, I'll get there as soon as I can."

He hung up, and Paige looked at him expectantly, guessing at what might be coming, but trying to will it not to be true.

When Christopher actually said the words, they hit Paige like a hammer.

"There's another body."

*

This was Paige's third crime scene, but she didn't think that she would ever get used to them, to the dread feeling that came as she approached them, knowing that inside, there was the body of someone Adam had killed.

This one was in a small suburban neighborhood, not wealthy by any means, but without the cramped, everyone piled on top of one another feeling that came with the inner city.

Although there were plenty of people around now, with the same crush of people there had been at the previous crime scenes Paige had been to. There were the police maintaining a cordon around the house, and the forensic techs working away steadily within that cordon, but there also seemed to be a greater number of reporters and photographers than there had been at either of the other scenes, along

122

with a fair number of people who were just standing around, obviously just trying to see what was happening.

"This is a lot of people," Paige said as they pulled up as close to the house as they could. With so many people there, not to mention all the police vehicles and TV vans, it wasn't as close as she might have hoped.

"It's turning into a circus," Christopher said. He didn't look happy about it.

"What do you mean?"

"The attention is spiraling out of control. With every day that passes, there's going to be more pressure to catch Riker. The story gets bigger, and the TV studios realize that they can get more airtime out of it. When we get out of the car, be careful what you say to anyone. Stay close to me and try not to stop for anything."

He made it sound as if they were walking into a war zone rather than just crossing the distance to the house.

Paige understood why he'd said that the moment she stepped out into the open air. Camera flashes started to go off all around her, bright enough that it was almost dizzying with its intensity. She'd thought that walking through the press at the first crime scene was bad, but this was far more intense.

Christopher's hand latched onto her arm, leading the way, helping to guide her through the press of it all.

Around Paige, a cacophony of questions burst out, the noise of the competing voices almost impossible to keep up with, so that the chaos of it all was almost as disorienting as the camera flashes.

"Agent Marriott, as the agent in charge of finding Adam Riker, what does it say about your efforts that he's now killed three people?"

"It just makes catching him even more important," Christopher fired back, continuing to move towards the house.

"Do you think that you're following the right lines of investigation?"

"In a case this important, we're following up on *every* line of investigation we can find," Christopher replied.

They were almost to the police tape now. Paige guessed that if they could just make it to the other side, they might have a little breathing space.

"Ms. King, why have you been brought in on the case? Do you really think you have anything to offer? Have you been leading the FBI on a wild goose chase?"

Paige whirled towards that reporter, anger flashing through her, partly at the question being directed towards her, but mostly because the question was far too close to the ones Paige had been asking herself.

"Does this bring back memories of your father?" another reporter asked. It seemed that they'd started to do their research on her.

This time, Paige couldn't help herself. "Leave my father out of this!"

Before she could say anything else, though, Christopher was there in between her and the reporter.

"Ms. King probably knows Adam Riker better than anyone else. Without her help, we wouldn't be as far along with this case as we are."

Paige was grateful for the defense, and even more grateful when Christopher led her to the far side of a line of police tape, into the open space beyond. There, Paige felt as though she could breathe properly again, and Christopher seemed to be willing to give her a moment or two to recover, as if he understood the intensity of what she'd just been through.

"You're probably wondering what they were talking about," Paige said, as she tried to recover. She knew that she was going to have to tell him all of it. "About my father."

"I have an idea," Christopher said. "But if you want to tell me yourself, you can."

Of course, the reporters wouldn't be the only ones to look her up. Paige knew that what had happened to her father sat between them unsaid. She had to be the one to say it.

"My father... was murdered," she said. "Killed by a serial killer who still hasn't been caught. I... I was the one who found his body."

She saw Christopher nod, even though he had to know already. "Thank you for telling me, Paige. I know none of this can be easy for you. Do you need more time to recover?"

Paige shook her head. It was better just to get on with this. They still had to head inside. As horrible as the last few moments had been, this was still the easy part compared to what was coming next. Paige knew that, but it didn't make it any easier to follow Christopher in there, into a neatly kept home with a couple of coats hanging from hooks in the hall and slightly worn brown carpet on the floor.

It was easy to guess by now where the body was, because that was the room with the highest concentration of forensic techs. Paige tried to steel herself as Christopher led the way inside. She knew what she was likely to see. She'd seen it before. Even so, it was hard to swallow back her shock as she saw the body, a woman contorted there until her body hadn't been able to breathe with it. There didn't seem to be any knife wounds this time, but that seemed crueler somehow. It would have been a slow, agonizing death this way.

Paige stared at her and couldn't look away. Not just because of the cruelty of it all. No, there was more to it than that. A slow, creeping sense of dread filled her, a kind of horror that wouldn't go away. There was one thing about this crime scene that she hadn't been expecting at all.

"Paige, what is it?" Christopher asked. "If you can't cope here…"

"I know this woman," Paige said, blurting the words out. "I know who she is. Her name is, *was,* Angelique. Angelique… Philips, I think."

"Another name from Adam's past?" Christopher said, obviously thinking that this was the same as Eloise Harper or Sara Langdon.

Paige shook her head. It wasn't the same, not even close. "Not his past, *mine*. We went to the same college. She… she started seeing one of my ex-boyfriends, straight after we broke up. I haven't thought about her in years."

She saw Christopher frown at that, as if he didn't quite understand. "Adam killed someone who went out with your boyfriend? Would he know that?"

"He would," Paige said. As she had so many times in investigating this, she felt so guilty in that moment, and so foolish. "We were talking in one of our sessions. I was trying to get him to talk about his relationships, and I gave him what I thought were details that didn't matter. I didn't even use Angelique's full name."

She tried to persuade herself that it hadn't been her fault, tried to repeat Christopher's reassurances to herself, but that was impossible with Angelique's dead body twisted there in front of her. Adam had done this because of what she'd said to him. She'd mentioned Angelique in their sessions, and now Angelique was dead.

Why had Adam done this? Why had he targeted someone in her life, rather than his own? Paige didn't know, but she *did* know that she couldn't be in that room anymore. Just the fact that he'd done this was too much for her. Far too much. Without wasting another moment, she ran for the backyard.

CHAPTER TWENTY ONE

Paige stood with her back to the rear wall of the house, wedged in between the house and the garage, trying to find a spot where the photographers wouldn't be able to get pictures of her.

She needed the support of the wall, of something that felt real, and solid. She felt as if she were having some kind of panic attack, breathing hard, having to force herself not to walk out of there completely.

Christopher was there then, and that was one more reason for Paige to feel guilty. He should have been back in the scene, doing his job, not looking after her.

"Paige, calm down. Talk to me."

Paige could barely find enough breath to say anything.

"Slow your breathing down," Christopher said. "Concentrate on my voice, if it helps."

It *did* help. There was something about having Christopher there that made Paige feel safe, although she knew that she should feel anything *but* safe, when Adam was targeting people she knew. When he'd already told her exactly how much he knew about her. He'd demonstrated what he knew, and even then, Paige had been able to hear the threat in his words. Now, that threat felt very personal.

Even so, she felt as if she shouldn't be wasting Christopher's time like this. He had much better things to do than stand out here, reminding Paige to breathe slower.

"You should be back in there, finding evidence," Paige said, when she was finally able to do it.

"Paige, you've just told me that you know that woman. I have plenty of forensics people in there who can tell me the details of what went on, but you're the only one who can tell me what this was about. You told me that she stole your boyfriend?"

Paige shook her head. That hadn't been how it was. "She didn't *steal* him, exactly. She just started seeing him right after. At the time, I was kind of pissed at her, but it wasn't a major thing. She didn't do anything wrong. She didn't do anything to deserve this."

Could *anyone* do anything that might deserve what Adam had done to Angelique? Paige couldn't imagine anything that could possibly warrant it. Angelique certainly hadn't done anything bad enough. She hadn't done anything wrong at all, really. Paige certainly hadn't had even a moment when she'd wished the woman back there dead. All that had happened was that she'd mentioned the events to Adam.

And he'd decided to act on them. He'd taken her words, and he'd turned them into a deadly kind of reality.

"That sounds like a pretty small thing," Christopher said. "It's worrying that Adam would kill someone over it."

"Think about what Adam said about his uncle." Paige tried to make some kind of sense of it all. "He told me that George Riker took part in the abuse he suffered. He blamed George, but what did George say to us?"

"That he'd never laid a finger on Adam, and that he'd only ever tried to help him," Christopher said. "So Adam blows things up out of nowhere?"

"Not completely out of nowhere," Paige explained. "It's like he has to have some small fragment to begin with, some small initial grievance. But in his mind, it becomes something much bigger. The same way that, in the institution, he would lash out if someone crossed him. I thought that was just him keeping to some kind of prison rules, but it's not, is it? It's a part of him ready to explode at any provocation."

Christopher nodded, and then looked at her levelly. "Feeling better?"

Paige realized what he'd done then, getting her to focus on the work, rather than on everything that she was feeling. She managed to nod.

"Good, then I need you to come back inside and tell me all about this."

"You need a statement, Agent Marriott?"

It all sounded far too formal. Paige wasn't sure that she was going to come out of this well.

Christopher held up a calming hand. "I just want you to talk to me. To explain what's going on. Come on, Paige, you know that I need to hear all of the details."

Paige understood. Of course, Christopher needed to hear all of it. He had to understand what was going on, or as much of it as Paige

127

could explain. She'd failed to help him so far, but maybe she could help with this part, at least.

Paige went with Christopher through to the kitchen of Angelique's house. There was a small table there, and the two of them took seats on either side of it. It was a long way from any kind of official interview room, but Paige still had the feeling that there ought to be a recording device down in between the two of them.

"Ok," Christopher said. "I need you to tell me it again. What's going on here? Angelique Philips is someone you know, and not Adam?"

"That's right," Paige said. "I didn't even really know her. I just mentioned her once in my sessions with Adam."

"And you think that he killed her because of that?" Christopher sounded worried.

"I… I don't know," Paige said. "He must have. I can't think of any reason he might have had of his own to kill her."

"So this is about the connection to you?" Christopher asked. "Come on, Paige. I know you're shocked by all this, but I need you to think. I need you to be the expert that I know you are. I need you to help me to understand what has happened here today."

"I… I can do that," Paige assured him.

"Good. I need to ask you a difficult question first, though," Christopher said.

Paige was still getting over her shock, but she was still thinking fast enough to guess what the next question had to be.

"You're going to ask me if I asked Adam to kill her, right? If I actually did help him to escape so that he could do this for me once he'd tied up his own loose ends. Maybe you even think that I've been leading you around to all these different places as a way to keep you from catching up to Adam before he could do this for me."

Christopher looked a little uncomfortable then.

"I don't think that, but I need to be able to justify you being here to my superiors when they ask. I need to be able to show that I asked the questions. It's my job, and I have to do it, even if I don't want to believe that you could ever do anything like that."

"I understand," Paige said, even though it hurt a little that he'd asked. It might be his job, but she wanted him to trust her. "So you need me to prove that I didn't have any part in this?"

Christopher nodded. "Because you're working with me, you have privileged access to the case." He sighed. "I trust you, Paige. I think you have more invested in catching Adam Riker than anyone else. I think you're the best person to work beside me on this. If I *didn't* think that, then I'd be working with someone else."

"But?"

"But I need to be able to tell anyone else who asks more than just 'I have a good feeling about her.'"

Paige guessed that she should be flattered that he had any kind of good feelings about her. It was still difficult to have to explain herself like this.

"The only interactions I had with Adam were in my sessions with him. I kept the audio files from every single one. You can hear for yourself that I never plotted anything with him, I never helped him. I just *didn't*."

Christopher spread his hands. "I believe you, Paige. I just needed to hear it. Now, I need to hear your opinion on why Adam has killed Angelique Philips. As the biggest expert on Adam Riker, tell me, why is he doing this?"

Paige didn't have an answer, which was embarrassing, because Christopher was right: she was meant to be the world's biggest expert on this one serial killer. She'd even thought that she'd managed to establish some kind of connection with him during their sessions.

What if he felt the same way? That thought crept over Paige, making her feel sick at the thought. What if Adam thought that they'd forged some kind of special connection, and now this was all about her?

"I think he's fixated on me," Paige said. She swallowed at the thought of it. "He told me in our last session that he knew all about my life. He told me that he would see me again. I thought it was a threat, but I hadn't imagined it would be anything like this."

Christopher nodded gravely. "It's a big shift in his MO. The first two murders since his escape seemed to be about his past. This shift to a focus on your life is worrying."

It was more than worrying for Paige. "What if he decides to use all the information he got from me in sessions? What if he decides to use everything he learned about me?"

"How *much* did he learn about you?" Christopher asked.

Paige wasn't sure, and that was terrifying in and of itself. "Is it possible that he's going to start killing people in my life? People I've mentioned in the sessions?"

She watched as Christopher nodded. "I wish I could tell you no, Paige. Do you know exactly what you told him?"

Paige wasn't sure. "I shouldn't have told him anything. I thought… I thought it was the only way to get him to start talking. It *was* the only way. I told him what I thought were small things, and he told me all about his life. I thought that it didn't matter, because he was safely locked away."

Looked at now, it seemed like a hideous risk, one that she should never have taken.

Christopher reached out, putting a hand over hers. Paige was grateful for that moment of physical contact, feeling an almost electric heat there between them.

"You couldn't have known what was going to happen. You tried to stop him from escaping. You tried to understand him. You aren't responsible for the actions of a psychopath, Paige."

"Except that in his head, I might be," Paige said. "If this has shifted to being about me, then I've put anyone around me in danger."

"*He's* the one doing that," Christopher reminded her. "Look, I need to go tell the local police about the potential new situation and check to see if there are any potential ways this crime scene can help us to find Riker before he does anything else. If we can catch him, then this is over."

"But you don't think it will be that simple," Paige said.

Christopher shook his head. "Which is why I need you to go through your notes again. I need you to work out exactly what you told him in your sessions, and who in your life he knows about. Once we know that, we can try to narrow it down, and know who we need to warn or protect."

Paige nodded. She could do that. She started to look through her notes. She couldn't listen to the recordings now, not here, not like this, but the transcripts were enough. Paige started to enter the names of the people close to her into the search bar, trying to find out which of them she'd talked about. Had she mentioned her mother, Prof. Thornton? Yes, they were both there, and just that fact was enough to make Paige feel sick all over again.

There were other places he might go too, but Paige *knew* that they needed to go to Prof. Thornton's house first, because of all the people she might have mentioned in her sessions, he was the nearest, and because he represented one of the best ways to get to Paige. She'd talked about him probably more than anyone in the sessions. He wasn't just her thesis supervisor; he was her mentor, her friend.

If Adam was targeting the people close to her, then Prof. Thornton could be in serious danger.

CHAPTER TWENTY TWO

They pulled up outside Prof. Thornton's house, with Paige hoping that they were in time. If something happened to the professor, Paige wouldn't be able to forgive herself.

Adam had to know that, too, which made it all the more likely that he would strike there.

That was why there was a local squad car following her and Christopher. He might not be able to swing another full stakeout just on Paige's say so, but he'd managed to pull police to keep an eye on the property.

Paige got out of the car, went up to the front door, and knocked. It was fifty-fifty whether the professor would be at home or at the university. She knew his schedule well enough to know that he didn't have any classes until this afternoon, but maybe he'd taken the opportunity to hit the library and do research in preparation for his next publication.

She breathed a sigh of relief as he answered the door, giving Paige a puzzled look.

"Paige? And Agent... Marriott, wasn't it? This is unexpected."

"May we come in, Professor?" Paige asked. "There's a problem. I think you might be in danger."

Something in her tone must have told the professor just how serious she was about that, because he stepped aside, waving her and Christopher inside, through to the living room.

"Take a seat, both of you," Prof. Thornton said.

Paige and Christopher both sat on the sofa, close enough that Paige could feel the weight of his presence there beside her. There was something comforting about that. There was also something comforting just about being back in this place.

"Now, what's all this about my being in danger?" Prof. Thornton asked, in a calm, soothing tone. It might as well have been a tutorial question: discuss the reasons that he was in danger, with examples.

"We believe that Adam Riker may try to target you, sir," Christopher said.

"And why do you believe that? Paige?"

Paige did her best to explain. "We've just come from a crime scene, another murder we think Adam is responsible for."

She saw Prof. Thornton nod. "I saw the news. I must say, I'm not entirely happy about you dragging one of my grad students around to crime scenes, Agent Marriott. Especially not when it has the press rooting around in issues that I'm sure must have caused Paige some distress when they brought them up."

The news had run with the stuff about her father, then. That made a familiar tightness clamp down in Paige's chest. She'd been through all of this before, with reporters hanging around, wanting to know exactly how she felt, caring more about their ratings than they ever did about what effect the questions had on Paige. She remembered as a child, having to essentially hide out in the wake of her father's murder, because neither she nor her mother had been able to stand one more question.

"I can handle it," Paige told the professor, although it took an effort to do it. Everything about this was hard, but she was a grown woman now. She wasn't going to hide away, the way she had as a kid. There was a reason that she'd gone into her field of study, trying to find answers rather than shying away.

"I hope that's true," Prof. Thornton said. "Now, what was there at this crime scene that makes you think that I might be a target?"

"The victim was Angelique Philips. She was a classmate of mine, back when I was an undergrad."

"And did she have any connection to Adam Riker?" Prof. Thornton asked.

Christopher answered that one. "None that we've been able to find. But she did start seeing one of Paige's old boyfriends."

"And Adam knows that because…"

"You've seen my session notes, Professor," Paige said. "I thought it was a good idea to give him something to get him to talk in return."

Prof. Thornton looked at Paige for several seconds. Was he judging her? Was he deciding that she wasn't fit to work with the worst of the worst after all? Was he already planning out the note that he would send to the university's ethics committee about Paige's actions?

"It's not your fault, Paige," he said, instead. "I imagine you're feeling quite guilty right now. You tend to take things on yourself that aren't yours to take."

"If I hadn't told Adam about Angelique-"

"Then he would have killed some other unfortunate. Someone would still be dead. Yes, telling Adam Riker personal details about yourself was… somewhat naïve, but I imagine it was founded on the reasonable calculation that he would never be in a position to do anything with the information." This was something Prof. Thornton was good at, assuaging Paige's fears about the way she was going with things. "There is one thing I still don't understand, though. Why does all of this lead you to think that I might be in danger?"

Paige tried to express it as best she could, knowing that the professor wouldn't be satisfied with a simple hunch.

"Adam's first two killings after he escaped were people from his past. Killing someone from *mine* makes me think that there has been a shift in his way of thinking. That he might have somehow… fixated on me in the institution. That he's decided to start killing people close to me. That might include you, my mother…"

"We can provide a couple of officers to watch your house until this is done," Christopher said. "Although it might be safer if you and your wife went somewhere else for a few days. Riker is dangerous enough that even police protection might not be enough."

Something about the seriousness of his tone must have gotten through to Prof. Thornton, because Paige saw the professor pale slightly at the prospect.

"Then I shall take Haley up to Lake Michigan for the weekend," Prof. Thornton said. "She has always liked it up there. Just to be on the safe side, you understand."

"That would make me feel a lot better," Paige said. She wanted to know that her mentor was safe, although there were plenty of other people who might still be in danger. She was going to have to call her mother, for one thing.

"Although I also believe that you may be mistaken," Prof. Thornton said.

Those words made Paige frown. "What do you mean?"

"You've decided that Adam Riker is targeting people close to you. Was Angelique Philips someone you were particularly close to?"

Paige stopped short. It was such a simple point, but in rushing to try to protect the people she cared about, she hadn't really considered it.

"No, she wasn't," Paige admitted.

"So what was she to you?" the professor asked.

"She was…" No, that wasn't quite the question, was it. "The real point is what Adam thinks she was to me, isn't it? He thinks that she's someone who did me this great wrong, even though it was nothing, really."

"Have *I* wronged you in some way that I don't know about?" Prof. Thornton asked.

Paige shook her head. "No, of course not."

He'd been a wonderful thesis supervisor. Without his guidance, Paige probably wouldn't have gotten through the work of her PhD.

"And do you feel that your mother wronged you?"

That was more complicated, because her mother had put her into one of the worst situations of her life. Yet she hadn't known what she was doing at the time, and Paige didn't blame her for it. The moment she'd found out, she'd gotten them both out of there.

"No."

"So why would Adam Riker come for either of us?" Prof. Thornton asked.

"He wouldn't, I guess." At least, Paige hoped that he wouldn't. She should have felt relief in that moment, except that Paige knew what the professor was driving at. She didn't want to go there, didn't want to think back to those moments.

"So who *has* wronged you, Paige?" Prof. Thornton asked. He said it gently, but he didn't let it go. He knew the answer, so Paige knew he was only asking the question because he needed her to say it aloud. "Who has done worse to you than anyone else? Worse even than the man who killed your father?"

Paige didn't want to say it. She didn't want to admit where she and Christopher needed to go next, because that would mean going there, and there was nothing that Paige wanted less in the world than to go to see this man.

"What is it?" Christopher asked. "Who do you think Riker is going to target next?"

Paige knew that she had to tell him. Even so, it was hard. Just saying it was hard.

"About three years after my father was murdered, my mother remarried, marrying a man named Jeremy Smithers. He… he seemed nice at first, but then, when my mother wasn't there… he came into my room…"

Even now, Paige could feel tears building in the corners of her eyes. The hurt didn't go away; it just got buried under the layers that she'd built up around it. And now she was supposed to go save this man? *Paige* wanted to kill him, most days.

Which was exactly why Adam would go after him.

CHAPTER TWENTY THREE

Going back to Jeremy Smithers's place was one of the hardest things that Paige had ever done in her life. It was a small house in an even smaller town out in Virginia, maybe an hour's drive away. When she and her mother had moved there, it had seemed like a huge new place to Paige, but now that she'd lived in D.C., the whole place just seemed like a backwater.

It wasn't anywhere that Paige had thought that she would visit again. One of her therapists had suggested it, and Paige hadn't been to see that therapist again. Driving there now felt like delving into an area of Paige's past that she didn't want to touch.

"Is it wrong that I hope we're too late when we get there?" Paige said. It wasn't entirely a joke. If Adam had to kill anyone in Paige's life, she found herself hoping that it would be her former stepfather.

"It's understandable," Christopher said, as they pulled off the main street of the small town, onto the street that held the old house. "Paige, you don't have to come in with me for this if you don't want to. I can deal with this."

Paige would have liked nothing more than to leave this to Christopher, but her every instinct told her that she needed to face up to this. She needed to show Jeremy that he didn't have any kind of power over her anymore.

When they pulled up outside the house, memories hit Paige of arriving there for the first time, but this wasn't quite the same place. It was more run down, with weeds growing out of control on the lawn. There were a couple of cracks in the woodwork that hadn't been there the last time Paige had been here. But then, that had been years, now.

Paige had to force herself to step out of the car, the memories threatening to come back as she stood there. Memories of moving in with her mother, seeing her happy. Memories of being in a new place, a new small town.

Memories of Jeremy, and what he'd done to her.

As if she could leave those memories in her wake, Paige strode up to the door and hammered on it. There was a doorbell, and Jeremy had always been very particular about people using it; it had been one of the

137

many things he'd gotten angry about. That was part of why Paige knocked so hard now.

Time had not been kind to Jeremy Smithers. He had to be around fifty now, but looked older, with wrinkles set in around his eyes and hair that was a dirty gray. He'd been handsome before, and proud of it. Those looks had been a part of what had lured Paige's mother in.

"You can't use a doorbell, you...," he tailed off, staring at Paige. "*You*. What are you doing here? Come to apologize for driving a wedge between me and your mother?"

"You think *I* should apologize to *you*?" Paige snapped back. "After what you did?"

"What did I do, Paige?" Jeremy asked. "Nothing you didn't want me to. Nothing you weren't *begging* me to do."

Paige hit him then. She couldn't hold back. She *didn't* hold back. She put her full weight into a punch that slammed into Jeremy's jaw, sending him crashing to the ground. It was the kind of punch she wished she'd been able to throw back when she was younger, back when he'd forced his way into her room, and abused her.

"You bitch, I'll-"

Christopher was there then, standing between them. Paige didn't know if that was to stop Paige from throwing any more punches or to protect her from Jeremy.

"Who's this?" Jeremy demanded as he struggled back to his feet. "Your boyfriend, here to protect you?"

Paige found herself half hoping that were true, but it wasn't, and it couldn't be. Besides, she didn't need protecting anymore.

Christopher flashed his ID then. "Agent Marriott, FBI."

"Then you should arrest this bitch for assaulting me!" Jeremy said. He seemed pretty brave now that Christopher was between Paige and him.

"From what I understand, it's you I should be arresting."

"For what?"

"For the sexual abuse of a minor," Christopher said, in a tone that made Jeremy take a step back.

"Oh, so you've set the FBI on me, have you, Paige? For what? What stories has she been telling you?" Jeremy had some of his bluster back again. "Shall I tell you what really happened? This little bitch destroyed my marriage. I was happy with her mother. *We* were happy, but she decided to start making up stories. And now she's doing it again."

138

Paige felt sick as he said it. Even now, he was lying about what happened, trying to make it sound as if she were making things up. He'd tried that back with her mother, trying to persuade her that Paige was a liar.

Thankfully, her mother had seen the truth. She'd left Jeremy, the two of them not looking back.

Paige glared at Jeremy with hatred.

"There's nothing you can do to me," Jeremy said. "Even if you arrest me, it's her word against mine."

The worst part was that it was probably true. It was why Paige had never tried to tell the police about him. Every facet of her life would be dragged through the mud; she would have to spend almost endless time in the legal system. It would tear her life apart, and what would happen in the end?

Nothing.

"And what's her word worth?" Jeremy said. "The girl who found her poor dead daddy. Who doesn't even know the full truth about his death."

Paige stood there staring at him, not knowing what to say in response to that. What did he mean? She didn't have enough time to ask, though, because Christopher was already speaking again.

"Mr. Smithers, we didn't come for that," Christopher said, although he sounded reluctant, as if he would have liked nothing more than to arrest Jeremy. Paige was grateful for that, but it didn't make any difference.

"Then why are you here?" Jeremy demanded. "Why have you brought that bitch to my home? Why did you come here, Paige?"

Paige was beginning to wonder that herself. It might have been far easier if she'd never told Christopher about Jeremy, if she'd just stood back and let Adam do everything that he wanted to the man who'd hurt her like that.

Even so, she couldn't. It wasn't about what he'd done. It was about what she chose to do now.

"We're here because a serial killer named Adam Riker may be targeting people who have wronged Paige here," Christopher said. "You're top of the list, Jeremy."

He said it in a tone that made it perfectly clear what he thought of Jeremy in that moment.

"Me? No, I'm not... I didn't *do* anything."

139

Paige couldn't hold herself back in that moment. She stepped past Christopher and hit Jeremy one more time. It felt almost as good as the first time that she'd struck him. He went down, hard.

"Paige, as much as I wish I could, I can't let you beat him."

"You should arrest her!" Jeremy insisted. "Arrest her!"

"For what? For defending herself when you made an aggressive move towards her when I went to arrest you?"

"When you *what*?" Jeremy demanded.

Christopher took a step forward, grabbing him and pushing him face first against a wall, none too gently. He got out handcuffs, and slapped them onto Jeremy's wrists, apparently not caring how tight they were.

"You can't do this!" Jeremy said.

"I can't arrest you for a crime you committed?" Christopher said.

"The charges will never stick! I'll be out in a day or two, at most!"

"Probably," Christopher said. "For all that you're a disgusting, child molesting scum, you're right about there not being enough supporting evidence to convict you. But there *is* enough to hold you for as long as we're allowed to question you. And while you're *being* questioned, you're probably safe from Adam Riker. You'd better hope that we catch him before you get out again."

It felt good to see Jeremy in cuffs, and even better as Christopher started dragging him to the car. The only pity was that there was no chance that he would be convicted, no chance that Paige would get to see him put away the way he deserved to be.

For now, it also meant that a man she would have gladly seen dead was going to get to live. Assuming that Adam was coming here. There was no sign of him here, and no obvious sign that he was going to show up. Were they going to sit here, the way they had at Adam's family home, waiting for the serial killer to show up?

No, Paige knew that there was no way that was going to happen, not after they'd struck out before. They might get local PD to watch it, but they couldn't stay. They *kept* striking out, and maybe they were protecting people who might be attacked, but that wasn't getting them Adam.

Paige needed to think of something else.

CHAPTER TWENTY FOUR

Paige was sick of running into dead ends. It seemed as if Adam were a ghost, always there on the edge of her vision, and with a presence she could almost feel, but was never quite there for her and Christopher to reach out and grab.

"How do you do it?" Paige asked, as she watched a local patrol car take away her stepfather.

"How do I do what? Lock up scumbags like that? That part's pretty easy. I just wish I could promise you that he would actually see any jail time."

Paige shrugged. "I resigned myself to that a long time ago. But no, I meant, 'how do you keep going when we've been wrong so many times?'"

Christopher put his hands on her shoulders. "That's just the job. You're wrong, over and over again, until you're right. Besides, we don't even know that you *are* wrong here. Adam isn't here right now, but that doesn't mean that he won't show up."

But they wouldn't be the ones there if he did. Maybe the local PD would keep an eye on her stepfather's place, but Paige and Christopher couldn't sit around again waiting for him. Paige could already see how doing that had given Adam time to get ahead of them both, moving on to his next victim each time.

He couldn't get to her stepfather now, however much Paige might wish he could, so who did that leave?

"You're saying that we just have to keep trying until we catch him?" Paige said. It sounded too much like the kind of advice a little league coach might have given to a kid from where she was standing.

"Sometimes you catch people through brilliant leaps and strokes of luck," Christopher said, "but honestly? The biggest advantage the FBI has is that we don't give up. We have the time and resources to keep grinding down a hunt like this until we find the person we're looking for."

"And how many people might Adam kill in the meantime?" Paige asked.

"Which is why we keep working to catch him, so that we find him as soon as it's possible to do so."

Paige wasn't entirely sold on that. For her, it felt as if this wasn't about just grinding down the evidence until she found Adam. It was about her guessing right or wrong, and so far, she'd been guessing wrong.

"I'm supposed to be the big expert on Adam," Paige said, "but I can't even predict what he's going to do next accurately."

"You will, it's just a matter of time," Christopher said.

They headed back to his car together, and once she was in the passenger seat, Paige got out her laptop, ready to go through her notes yet again, trying to find another angle that might lead the two of them to the serial killer they were hunting.

To her surprise, though, Christopher reached out and closed the laptop.

"What are you doing?" Paige demanded. "I thought you wanted me to take another shot at finding Adam."

Christopher nodded as he put the car in gear. "I do, but maybe this time, don't spend all your time looking through your sessions, trying to find that one hint that will lead you to him."

That didn't make any sense at all to Paige. "Then how am I even going to begin to find him?"

"I didn't bring you along with me just because of your notes," Christopher replied as they started to drive back through the town, heading back along the roads that would take them to D.C. again. "I could have had you copy those over to me so that a team of FBI analysts could go through them. I *have* people who can do that. What I don't have is someone who knows Adam. Who has sat in the same room as him and looked him in the eyes."

"You work with the BAU," Paige pointed out. "You must know that looking people in the eyes doesn't actually tell you anything."

"You know what I mean, Paige," Christopher insisted. "I don't just want what's in your notes. I want your expertise, and the knowledge that you've built up. They had you working with people like Adam for a reason. You started studying him for a reason."

Yes, because of everything that had been taken from her by someone just like him. Someone who didn't care about anyone else, or anything else, except…

Except *her,* in Adam's case. He'd fixated on Paige. He'd sat there and told her about himself.

142

"You know that he knew exactly what he was telling me," Paige said. "Anything I remember, he'll also remember."

"Then don't just try to remember," Christopher replied, as they kept driving. "Tell me about him. *Profile* him."

"Adam is…," Paige tried to find a way to put it into words. All this time working on her PhD, and it still didn't feel as if she had the essence of him. "He's controlling, he's manipulative. He reacts poorly to slights, because he thinks that if he lets anyone get away with even small stuff, it makes him look weaker. He seems to have fixated on me, seems to be trying to do for me what he does with people who have wronged him, but I'm not sure what that gets us. It makes Jeremy the most obvious target, but I'm not sure who else it might be. It isn't as if I have a long list of enemies."

Paige kept thinking, trying to focus on Adam, trying to get deeper into his thought processes. He'd killed Eloise Harper because she was unfinished business for him, and Sara Langdon because… well, because he'd shifted his attentions to Paige, and there was no reason for him to keep her alive anymore. He'd killed Angelique because of something that she'd done to Paige, so logically, her stepfather should have been the next victim. So where had she gone wrong?

"At least you got the chance to punch your stepfather," Christopher said. "Not that I should approve, of course. But you do have a pretty good right cross."

"Thanks."

That was one good point about this: punching Jeremy had been at least vaguely cathartic. Strangely, hitting him the second time hadn't felt quite as good as the first, with a kind of diminishing return that came from knowing that nothing would ever happen to him, really, for what he'd done.

"The hardest part was when he tried to make out that it was all in my head. He treated it all as if he hadn't done anything wrong."

"Does he actually believe that, do you think?" Christopher asked.

Paige was about to reply when something snagged in her brain. A flicker of something that made her sit staring while she tried to work it out.

"I'm sorry, I've said the wrong thing," Christopher said.

"No, the *right* thing," Paige tried to latch onto the thought, and when it came to her, it was breathtakingly obvious. "This is about belief."

"I didn't think Adam was religious."

143

Paige was already shaking her head. "Not that kind of belief. I mean, it doesn't matter what's true. It only matters what Adam believes to be true. When he spoke about his uncle helping to abuse him, it doesn't matter if that was true or not, only that he thought it was. And when he killed Angelique, it doesn't matter that I never thought of her as having done me some great wrong, only that *he* did."

"So what does that mean for the case?" Christopher asked as he neatly overtook another car, glancing across at her.

Paige tried to take in all the implications. "It means that Prof. Thornton was wrong earlier. He told me that I had to focus on Jeremy because he was the person who had most obviously wronged me. But in Adam's mind, it could be someone else entirely. Someone who never did anything wrong but who he thinks did."

"Who?" Christopher asked, a sense of urgency in his voice. "If he's about to strike again, Paige, I need to know who he's going to attack."

Now, there was no sense of it being ok if Paige guessed wrong, no sense that they could just keep trying until they caught Adam. Now, she could hear how much he needed her to get this right, because as much as he'd tried to tell her that it was all ok, someone's life hung in the balance.

Who, though? Someone connected to Paige, obviously. Someone Adam thought had done her wrong, presumably because Paige had mentioned them in their sessions.

One name leapt out from Paige's memories instantly. "My mother. He's going to target my mother."

"Are you sure?" Christopher asked.

There was no room this time to get things wrong.

"He knows I don't have a great relationship with my mother after everything that happened. I'm sure I talked about things being wrong with her at one point, to try to get him to open up…"

Paige could remember the conversation perfectly. She'd mentioned her mother, trying to get Adam to open up about his uncle. If Adam thought that they were essentially the same, if he thought that she was somehow guilty for not spotting the abuse that Jeremy had inflicted on Paige in time…

"It's her, Christopher. He's going to kill my mother."

"Where is she now?" Christopher asked.

"A couple of towns over, back the way we came."

Paige felt the car lurch as Christopher skidded to a halt and spun it around. A car behind them hit its horn, barely stopping in time before it

144

hit them. Paige didn't care right then. The only thing that mattered was getting to her mother in time.

CHAPTER TWENTY FIVE

From his hiding place across the street, Adam watched Vivien King. He stared through the windows of her home, eyes following her as she made what seemed to be a pie in the kitchen. She looked a lot like her daughter, with the same petite frame, the same red hair, just fading a little with age now. She was a perfect vision of homemaking bliss there.

She didn't deserve it.

She didn't deserve anything, after what she'd done to Paige.

Adam started to edge forward, towards the house, trying to make it look as if he were simply a stranger out for a walk, while hiding the cold fury that powered him.

A mother's task was to protect her child, just as Adam's mother should have protected him from the beatings, rather than leaving. *This* one had stayed, but that hadn't done anything to stop the things Paige's stepfather had done to her. She'd been willfully blind, let her supposed love for the man override the need to protect her daughter.

Adam kept moving forward, walking along in front of the house, wanting to pick his moment. He didn't want to approach it directly, because that would have let her see him coming, given her time to run.

Adam had told Paige in their final session that empathy was a lie, that it was impossible to truly know what the world was like for another person, yet in this case, he understood Paige perfectly. It was just one part of what made the connection between them so strong.

Adam swung down the side of the house, moving a little quicker now. He could be seen from the street or the surrounding houses for a second or two, and this was the kind of neighborhood where people might call the police if they saw him doing that, or even come out to challenge him.

Adam didn't want to be interrupted before he finished what he'd come here to do. This was the moment that mattered.

He'd thought about killing the stepfather who'd hurt her, but Adam had guessed that Paige would be waiting there with the FBI. Besides, she'd already broken away from him emotionally. *This* woman still seemed to exert some kind of hold over her. Paige acted as if she didn't blame her mother, when Adam knew that the horror of her actions had to be eating Paige up inside.

He'd killed Angelique Philips for the same reason: *he'd* seen the pain that she'd caused Paige, even if Paige did her best to hide it and pretend that it was nothing. Adam had made that right the way he made every wound done to him right. He'd done it both for Paige and to show her just how deeply he was thinking of her.

Her mother was the next step. Adam knew that Paige would never do this herself. At least, not yet. He hoped that if he showed her what was possible, she might see that she had the power to act herself.

His plan was to show her who she could be, who she really was.

She might see that they weren't so different after all.

Adam was at the side door to the house now. He paused, taking out his lockpicks, starting to work on the lock silently, feeling for the give of the tumblers. This was always a tense moment, a moment when he could be caught, obviously committing a crime, but before he had achieved what he came to do.

Adam didn't feel really fear, though. He liked to think that Paige wouldn't either, in his position. Adam had thought that Sara Langdon was the same as him, but their connection had turned out to be a false thing, a lie. He'd seen the truth now: that it should always have been Paige in his heart, rather than her.

Adam felt the lock give way under his efforts, with the softest of clicks. He pushed the door open slowly and silently, giving him a way into the house.

Adam dared to dream of the future in that moment: of him and Paige together. He'd seen how special she could be over the course of their sessions together. He'd seen the potential there.

The potential to be like him. The potential to be everything he was.

Adam padded into the house, making his way towards the kitchen on silent feet. As he did so, it was impossible not to imagine Paige padding beside him, stalking her mother even as he did. Perhaps one day, she would.

At first, her thesis had held no interest to him. Trying to understand what made him a killer? Why should he help her do something like that? Yet, as things had gone on, as he'd started to learn about her life, Adam had started to see the parallels: someone young, who had been abused, who had lost one parent, and found the other a part of that abuse. Someone intelligent, charismatic, who had found her own way through the world in spite of everything that had happened.

147

Adam had found himself fascinated by that, by the question of how someone could be so similar to him, yet on the other side of the conversation, asking about serial killers rather than being one herself. He found himself asking what the difference was.

He was in the kitchen now, Vivien King just a pace or two away. Adam waited for his moment, wanting her to be far enough from anything that might hurt him before he struck. He found himself thinking that Paige would admire his patience.

He'd come to the conclusion with Paige that there *was* no difference between the two of them. That she had all the potential needed to be just like him. She simply needed the right push. And then... the two of them could truly be together. They could do whatever they wanted. They could *kill* whoever they wanted.

Paige would see that soon. He would *make* her see that.

First, though, Adam had to do this. He saw Paige's mother take a step back from the counter, and that was when he struck. He lunged forward, his forearm going around her neck, his hand putting a chemically soaked cloth over her mouth as he dragged her back off balance. Vivien had a moment to cry out, but then his arm was dragging back sharply into her throat, cutting off both the sound and the air that she needed to make it.

He had no doubt that Paige would be shocked by this. Perhaps she would even be upset. Yet she would see that this was necessary. This was her doorway into what she needed to become.

Adam kept his grip as Vivien King struggled, continuing to drag her back off balance because that made it harder for her to fight. He felt her struggles starting to weaken, her limbs slowly going slack as the sedative took effect.

She went still and Adam let her go, unconscious, but not yet dead. He took out a rope and started to bind her hands.

He didn't put her in a position that would eventually suffocate her, though. Not yet. It was a big change for Adam. Normally, he killed his victims in the places where he took them. The location didn't matter so long as it was secure enough that he wouldn't be disturbed.

This was a special case, though. He was doing this for Paige, and that meant that he had to do this in a way that would mean something to her. He would take her mother's car for this. It would make her easier to find.

Picking up Vivien King, he took her to her car and used her keys to unlock it. He shoved her into the trunk, and then headed back into the

148

house, looking for Vivien's phone. When he found it, he did something that he had never done at the scene of one of his killings, and dialed 911.

He waited for an operator to pick up.

"911, which service do you require?"

Adam didn't bother with that part. He was sure that his message would get where it needed to go. "This is Adam Riker. Tell Paige King that I'm at her mother's house. Tell her that I will be at the last spot she lost someone."

CHAPTER TWENTY SIX

They were driving at speeds that would ordinarily have scared Paige, but right then the possibility of something happening to her mother frightened her far more. The landscape flashed past outside, and Paige tried to keep up with it so that she could give Christopher meaningful directions to her mother's house.

"Left up here. Yes, we're almost at the town."

They flashed past cars as they drove. Thankfully, the roads out here were pretty quiet, and Christopher had both his lights flashing and a siren running, but even so, Paige felt sure that they were going to crash into one at some point.

Christopher's face seemed to be a picture of concentration as he drove. He'd obviously had training in this kind of high-speed driving. At least, Paige hoped that he had. The thought that he might just be winging this only made the whole situation more terrifying.

"Call your mother," Christopher told her, as they skidded around the corner that Paige had indicated.

Paige took out her phone and did it, hoping that her mom would pick up. Maybe she would be able to warn her, to tell her to get out of the house and go over to a neighbor, or to wait for them in a public place. The last place her mom should be was inside, alone. That was exactly where Adam liked to murder his victims. She needed to be where he couldn't get to her without it being public and obvious.

The phone rang and rang… then clicked over to voicemail.

"Mom, it's me," Paige said. "If you're there, pick up right now."

Her mom didn't pick up, though. Paige tried again, then again, telling herself each time that it might just be that her mom had put her phone down somewhere while she was off doing something else. She might be in another room, or have her phone on silent, so that she wasn't hearing the calls.

Paige wanted to believe that was true, but her fears told her that there was another, far worse explanation. Her mom not answering might mean that Adam was right there with her, killing her even while Paige tried to get through to her. The thought of that was terrifying, making Paige feel sick with worry for her mother.

150

She didn't know what she would do if anything happened to her mother. She'd been there for Paige through so much, even if she didn't really understand Paige's obsession with serial killers now. The thought of losing her was almost too much to bear.

They'd reached the town now, and Paige had to put the phone down so that she could give directions to Christopher.

"Right here, then left. Yes, just here."

They wove through the thankfully light traffic of the town, following Paige's directions, heading for the home that she'd shared with her mother after they'd gotten away from Jeremy and his place.

"Just down this street," Paige said, "right at the end there."

Even as she said it, Paige saw the police cars parked there at an angle in the street and a shocked kind of horror hit her like a punch to the stomach. If the police were there, then...

"No," Paige said. "No. We can't be too late. We can't!"

"We don't know what's happened yet," Christopher said, as they pulled to a halt. His tone was obviously aiming for comforting, but Paige could hear the worry there behind it. He was as worried as she was that they were too late.

They were too late, and now her mother might be in there, tangled up and killed by Adam. Paige could picture it all too easily, now that she'd been in the other crime scenes linked to Adam, now that she'd seen *exactly* what he could do, close up. Just reading a few files and looking at a few pictures for her thesis wasn't the same thing.

"Come on, Paige," Christopher said, getting out of the car.

Paige had to force herself to follow him. She didn't *want* to follow him, didn't want to see what was in there as he made his way over to a couple of local cops standing by their car, speaking urgently into their radios.

Christopher was with them now, showing them his ID as he started to explain who he was.

As they started to respond, Paige realized that she'd been wrong just a moment or two ago. Then, she hadn't wanted to see what was happening. Now, inexplicably, she did. She had to see it for herself, had to know, one way or another. She couldn't wait around, be told about her mother's death, and only then get to see what had happened. Or worse, not be allowed to see it at all so that her imagination would have to fill in every horrific detail.

So Paige ran for the door, instead. The front door was closed, but Paige guessed that Adam would have gotten in around the side.

"Paige, wait!" Christopher called after her, but Paige didn't slow down.

The back door was open, a local police officer kneeling near it, apparently trying to collect evidence. Paige was past him before he could react, and then through, looking around the place, trying to see what had happened to her mother.

There was no sign of her in the kitchen, nor in the living room. Paige was making her way to the stairs when Christopher caught up to her, grabbing her around the waist and holding her back. Under other circumstances, Paige might have given a lot to be that close to the handsome FBI agent, but right now, she struggled to try to get free.

"She isn't here, Paige," Christopher said. "She isn't here."

The words cut through the sense of panic that filled Paige at the thought of her mother being dead, making her stop cold. She turned to face him, expecting to find some hint of hope and reassurance there, but Christopher's expression was still grave.

"You're sure? What is it, Christopher?"

"Come outside and hear it for yourself."

He led the way back outside, in the direction of the squad cars. The police officers were waiting there, managing to look both disapproving that Paige had run into the house and sympathetic about the reasons why she might have done it.

"Can you tell my colleague what you started to tell me before she ran inside?" Christopher asked one of the officers. He was a bulky, middle-aged man with a short beard. His name badge said that he was Officer Lane.

"We arrived about ten minutes ago. We found that the house had been broken into, with no sign of the homeowner. Her vehicle appears to be missing, and we have reason to believe that Adam Riker might have been here."

Paige was about to ask what reason, but she realized that there was only one way that the police could have been there when she and Christopher arrived.

"Someone called you? Someone saw this happen?"

The police officer looked uncomfortable for a moment or two. "Someone claiming to be Adam Riker called 911, telling us that he was here."

He'd called the police? That didn't make any sense to Paige. She looked over to Christopher.

"This doesn't fit with what Adam does," she said. "He breaks into a house, or an office, or somewhere, and he kills his victims there. He doesn't... what *did* he do? Shove my mother into her car and drive her somewhere else?"

"I don't know," Christopher said. "It's a big shift in his MO, but so was his last killing. He's doing something else here, and maybe he decided that he needed to be somewhere else in order to do it. There's one piece of good news, though, Paige."

"What could possibly be good about any of this?" Paige demanded.

"That he's taken your mother rather than killing her straight away," Christopher said.

As consolations went, it felt like a very slender one to Paige.

"Wait, you're Paige King?" Officer Lane asked.

Paige nodded. "Yes, why?"

"The man claiming to be Adam Riker mentioned you in his message," Officer Lane said. He looked over to Christopher, as if wanting to confirm that telling her was the right thing to do.

"Just tell us," Christopher said.

"The message said to tell Paige King that he had taken her mother, and that she would find her in the last spot she lost someone."

Almost as soon as the police officer said it, Paige knew where Adam was taking her mother. If he knew about her, then he knew that there was one spot that meant more in Paige's life than any other, one spot that had changed everything for her.

"What does it mean, Paige?" Christopher asked. "It's obvious that he thinks you know where he means."

Paige nodded. She knew. There was no way of not knowing. This was one location that would forever be burned onto Paige's memory.

"He's taking her to the spot where I found my father's body."

CHAPTER TWENTY SEVEN

Paige had hoped never to see this particular patch of woodland again. It was a local beauty spot, with a babbling stream and clearings filled with wildflowers, but for Paige, there could never be anything beautiful about it now. Not when every memory she had of it was bound up with the sight of her father's corpse, there on the floor of the forest.

She and Christopher pulled up in a parking lot/picnic area that formed the starting point for a couple of the walking trails through the wood. In summer, on a holiday, the place would have been packed with people, but now it was pretty much empty.

Paige felt a thread of cold fury as she saw her mother's car, but also a hint of satisfaction that at least they were in the right place.

"He's here with her," she said.

"Then we need to call in backup," Christopher said. "I can have a tactical team here in twenty, and the local cops here in ten."

"And what happens to my mother in the meantime?" Paige asked. She had another thought. "What happens when Adam hears that tactical team coming?"

Christopher gave her a serious look. "I don't know, but it's the safest way to do this, Paige."

Paige shook her head. "Not for my mother. You've said all along that I'm the one who knows Adam; well, I know what he'll do if he's startled. He'll kill her without a second thought, and then disappear into the woods. We'll never find him, even with more people on the ground."

She knew how much Christopher wanted to catch Adam, and she also guessed that he wanted to protect her mother. Neither of those things would be served by calling in backup.

She saw Christopher look away for a moment, but then nod tersely.

"Ok. It's not procedure but protecting your mother's life has to come first."

"This is your best chance to catch Adam, too," Paige said. "We know where he is at last. We can't risk him running because he thinks something is wrong."

Christopher seemed determined in that moment. "All right. I'm going to call backup, just in case this goes wrong, but after that, we'll approach and try to resolve this without your mother being hurt."

Paige knew that she couldn't argue with that. She also knew that they couldn't afford to waste any time with her mother's life at stake.

Christopher made a call. "This is Agent Marriott. I'm requesting urgent backup to my location. Adam Riker is here, and he appears to have a hostage."

He hung up. "They're on their way. Lead the way to the spot."

Paige hoped against hope that they would be able to save her mother before this turned into something even more deadly. She started to lead the way through the woods, her memory providing the route along the walking paths all too easily. She hadn't walked this way in over a decade, hadn't been able to bear being here, but the path was still burned into her brain indelibly by what had happened here.

The first part was easy, because it just meant following a couple of the trails deeper into the woods. There were markers along the route so that hikers and nature lovers could orient themselves, but Paige found herself using much older markers: a great oak that she had climbed as a girl, a twist in the path that she remembered having no reason to it, until she'd looked and found the stump of a tree, covered in undergrowth.

"Do you think that Adam will still be there?" Christopher asked. "Do you think he even knows the right spot to wait?"

Paige could hear the worry there, and it echoed some of her own worries. Every moment this took was one in which Adam might decide that he was bored of his new way of doing things, and might decide to kill her mother, then slip away. Paige had to tell herself that he wouldn't do that, though.

"This is about me," she said. "He took my mother to draw me in. That doesn't work if he isn't waiting at the end of all of this. And he'll know the spot. He'll have made sure that he does."

"Yes, but what is he waiting to do?" Christopher asked.

Paige wasn't sure about that part. She *thought* that Adam wanted to talk, that he'd gotten her attention, and now he wanted to show her how much he'd done for her, at least in his mind. But it was also possible that he was doing all of this to lure Paige in. It was possible that he'd seen that she was working with the FBI, and now he thought that the best way to get to her and to kill her was to take her mother from her.

For all Paige knew, she could be walking straight into a trap.

155

Even so, she kept walking, leading the way down the trail to a marker that she knew far too well. It had been this marker where she'd left the trail all those years ago, this marker that had eventually led to her staring down at her father's body, at the work of a serial killer.

Was she going to find herself staring at her mother's body the same way today? Paige hoped not, with every fiber of her being. She couldn't stand the thought of her mother being hurt, certainly not here, like this.

Paige was so caught up in her thoughts that for a moment or two, she didn't notice the note pinned to the trail marker. It read simply *Paige, come alone.*

Paige picked it up and stared at it. The demand was simple and clear, the threat implicit. If she didn't do what Adam wanted, then there was every chance that he would murder her mother. If she did...

"No way are we doing what this psycho wants," Christopher said.

"I might have to," Paige insisted.

"What? No, no way."

Christopher sounded determined, but Paige was just as determined, in her way. She wasn't about to let her mother be killed.

"If you come with me, then you know Adam will kill my mother the moment he sees you."

"We don't know that for certain."

Paige fixed him with a level look. "*I* know it, and I know Adam. You need to hang back."

"And just let you walk into danger alone? That's not going to happen. Facing down a serial killer isn't your job, Paige."

Paige offered him a faint smile. "Being face to face with Adam has been my job for a while now. He wants to talk, Christopher."

"So what, you're planning to talk down a man who has killed three people since breaking out of a secure mental hospital? He'll kill you."

Paige shook her head. "I don't think that he will. Certainly not straight away. He wants something from me, so I go to him, and I talk to him. You can follow, and maybe the distraction will mean that he doesn't see you, but if you come with me, my mother *will* die."

Paige was more certain of that than she had been of anything else in her life. She couldn't let Christopher come with her on this. The problem was that the only tool she had to stop him was words.

"I'll be ok," Paige told him. "I know what I'm doing with this."

She did, or she thought she did, at least. Certainly, it was better than any of the alternatives. She could do this. She had to.

156

Christopher must have heard some of the confidence in her words, because he held up his hands. "All right. But I'm going to follow. And *you're* going to take this."

He took out his service weapon, handing it to her. Paige stared at it, and at him, in surprise.

"You want me to take your gun? But *you'll* need it. And besides, I'm pretty sure you're not meant to just give someone your gun, Christopher. You're an FBI agent."

"And *you're* the one who's walking into a potentially deadly situation," Christopher replied. "I don't care if I lose my job over this. My weapon does no good if it's a hundred yards back, with me. With you, it might give you a chance. And if it comes to taking Riker down, I can do that hand to hand if I have to."

"Christopher-" Paige began, but the FBI agent was already shaking his head.

"No, this is not negotiable. Either you take the weapon, or you don't go."

There was no give in his voice, so Paige took the gun, tucking it into her waistband in the absence of a holster. She pulled her shirt down over it, hoping to hide its presence.

Christopher hugged her then. Paige was pretty sure that was something FBI agents didn't normally do, either.

"Good luck," he said.

"Thanks."

Paige set off into the trees, finding her way by memory. Every step was another back along the path she'd taken as a girl, looking through the woods. A fallen tree she remembered had been cleared now, but a small mound was still there, and a cluster of rocks that had been balanced there by someone unknown years before. Step by step, Paige made her way to the small clearing where she had found her father's body.

If it weren't for the memories Paige had of the clearing, it would have been beautiful. A carpet of wildflowers filled it, with a single birch tree at the center, standing apart from the rest of the forest in a space of its own.

Adam stood there next to it, as calmly as if he had been waiting to meet a friend for coffee. He was wearing dark jeans and a hooded top, and a hunting knife rested almost casually in his right hand.

Paige's mother stood bound to the tree, ropes holding her to it like some giant spider's web. More ropes ran across her mouth, in a

157

makeshift gag. Her eyes were open and she was still breathing, which made a flood of relief flow through Paige; but right then, she couldn't relax. This was still a deadly situation.

"There you are, Paige," Adam said. "We've been waiting for you. I trust you came alone? I'd hate to have to slit your mother's throat and run because you didn't."

"I came alone," Paige lied, hoping that Christopher was far enough back that Adam wouldn't be able to tell the difference.

"That's good." Adam smiled now, as he gestured to Paige's mother. "I have a gift for you, Paige."

"My mother isn't a gift you can give me," Paige replied.

"No, but her death is. I know how you must hate her, Paige, for what she did. For what she *failed* to do. She stood by while you were abused. She let it happen. The only reason she is still alive is because... well, I knew that you would want to tell her exactly what you really feel about her before we end this. Together."

CHAPTER TWENTY EIGHT

Paige could only stand there, staring at Adam as he stood in front of the tree to which Paige's mother was bound like some kind of offering. Which was exactly what he clearly intended her to be. An offering to Paige, for her to kill.

"I don't want to kill my mother, Adam," Paige said.

Adam laughed then. "Of course you do, Paige. You just won't admit it to yourself. But that's all right, because I'm here."

He said it as if that were meant to be a comfort, rather than a source of terror for both Paige and her mother.

"I know how carefully you listened in our sessions," Adam said. "I know you tried everything you could to understand me. But I was learning to understand you at the same time."

"And what have you understood, Adam?" Paige asked, trying to buy time. She wondered if she should pull Christopher's gun now but doing that robbed her of any chance to try to end this situation peacefully. What had Christopher told her? Not to point it at anything she didn't intend to kill? Well, even now, Paige wasn't sure if she would be able to kill Adam.

"That we're the same," Adam said. "That we have all the same experiences, the same background. The only difference is that I killed my first person when I was still fairly young, so it came easily to me. I understand that it's harder for you."

"I'm not going to kill anyone, Adam," Paige said.

She saw her mother struggling against the ropes that held her, obviously unable to get loose.

Adam just smiled wider. "Of course you are. I did this for you, Paige. To show you everything that you could be. I see you have a gun. Why don't you take it out?"

Paige obviously hadn't done a very good job of concealing the weapon after all.

"Take out the gun, Paige," Adam said, in a harder tone. He lifted the knife slightly. "Do it. I've gone to a lot of trouble for you, and you're going to do your part."

159

He started to take a step towards Paige, and in that moment, she *did* pull the gun, holding it braced and two handed, exactly the way that Christopher had shown her.

Adam smiled, then.

"That's better. *Much* better. Now, would you like to shoot your mother? Be honest, now."

"I'd rather shoot you," Paige said.

"Would you?" Adam countered. "Then why haven't you done it already? No, the truth is that you know I have only done you favors, while your mother contributed to some of the worst moments of your life. To moments that made you feel weak and helpless, completely out of control, the way I did whenever my father beat me."

Memories threatened to overtake Paige then, threatened to well up inside her and leave no room for anything else. In that moment, she was back there in her room, and her stepfather was coming in, and...

"No," Paige said, forcing down the memories. "You don't get to do this to me, Adam. You don't get to control me. I'll-"

"You'll what, Paige? Kill me? Go on then. Do it."

Paige stood there with the pistol trained on him, hand shaking slightly.

"*Do it!*" Adam roared at her. "Do it, if you think you have it in you. Show me what you can do. Show me what you really are."

He wanted her to shoot him?

"Shoot me, or I'll kill her," Adam said, gesturing with the knife at Paige's mother, as she stood there, pinned against the tree by his ropes. "If you can't stand the thought of killing her yourself, then I'll do it. And then... well, you will have disappointed me."

And he would kill Paige afterwards.

"You have three choices, Paige," Adam said. "You can shoot your mother, you can shoot me, or you can stand by and be a victim for what's left of your life."

With those words, he lunged towards the tree, and Paige's mother.

Paige pulled the trigger before she could even think about it.

The roar of the gun was an explosion of sound against the silence of the forest. Paige saw Adam stumble, his knife gone from his grasp as he fell to his knees.

Paige stood over him, then, the weapon pointed down at his skull. She hated him in that moment, hated him for everything he'd done, and for the ways in which he'd manipulated her. She hated this man who had killed so many people, and who had tried to kill her mother.

160

Even now, Adam looked up at her with something approaching triumph.

"Do it," he breathed. "*Do it,* Paige."

Paige could feel her finger tightening on the trigger again. She wanted to do this. She wanted to rid the world of an evil man. She wanted to stop Adam, once and for all.

The only thing that stopped her was the thought that he wanted it, too.

He was looking up at her like he was proud of her. Like he still thought that there was some kind of special connection between them. Paige understood then that it didn't matter to Adam whether she killed him. It might even have been a part of what he'd been hoping would happen here today.

Some part of him must have known that the odds of getting away for long were poor. That with the full might of the FBI hunting him and his picture on every news channel, he would be spotted sooner or later.

"You want this, don't you?" Paige said. "You're trying to turn me into someone like you."

"You *are* someone like me, Paige," he said. "You just haven't seen it yet. I thought that I could show you, and we'd be together. Now, I know that you'll be my legacy to the world."

"You're manipulating me, even now," Paige said. She pressed the barrel of the gun to his forehead. That fact made her hate him all the more.

But it also made her want to beat him, not just kill him. If she shot Adam now, he'd won. He'd succeeded in turning her into a cold-blooded killer. Paige couldn't let him do that.

So she stepped back and lowered the gun.

Adam snarled at her like an animal, surging up to his feet as if he might attack her even then, obviously trying to force her to end it.

Christopher was there then, though, sprinting into the clearing as if he'd run all the way in the seconds since the sound of the gunshot, slamming into Adam with his full weight. The two of them went down to the ground in a heap, Christopher landing on top.

Adam struck back at him, lashing out with the knife he had grabbed. If there hadn't been the weapon, then he would have had no chance, wounded as he was, but its presence meant that Christopher had to grab for it with both hands, locking onto it to stop himself from being stabbed, while Adam struck out at him with head, knees, and even teeth.

Paige saw Christopher strike back, the two of them rolling over in the dirt of the forest floor. Paige still had the gun, but there was no way that she could risk a shot with the two of them tangled so close.

She could, however, step in and reach for Adam. She grabbed him, closing her grip on his wounded shoulder, and he screamed with it. The knife fell from his grasp, and Paige kicked it away.

Christopher was on top of Adam then, rising up and punching him once, twice, a third time. It wasn't a fair fight anymore. It wasn't even close. Wounded as he was, Adam had no chance to out-fight the FBI agent.

Christopher wrenched him over onto his stomach, not showing any sign of caring as Adam howled in pain. He took out a set of handcuffs, slapping them on Adam's wrists.

It was finally over.

"Adam Riker, you are under arrest."

CHAPTER TWENTY NINE

Paige went with her mom to the hospital to get her checked out, sitting by her bedside as a young doctor looked her over. Paige kept one eye on the door, because she was pretty sure that there would be journalists here sooner or later, trying to get the full story of what had gone on.

"You seem to be physically ok, Mrs. King," the doctor said, taking a step back from Paige's mother. "You have some bruises, and I imagine you will be sore for several days to come, but I don't believe that you have suffered any major injuries. I'd like to keep you in for an hour or two for further observation, but after that, you should be free to go. I can put you in touch with a counselor if you would like."

"No, thank you," her mother replied, but that had always been her way. Even while Paige had been seeing a therapist about her father's death, her mother had never spoken to anyone about it all.

The doctor left, which meant that Paige and her mother were alone in the room together, Paige sitting by the side of her mother's bed and staring at her.

"I heard the things that man said," her mother said after a while. There were tears at the corners of her eyes. "About what happened with Jeremy. About how I failed you with him."

"Mom, he was wrong," Paige said, putting a hand over her mother's.

Her mother shook her head, though. "No, sweetheart, he wasn't. I should have done more. I should have seen what kind of man Jeremy was. I should have protected you. Every time I see you, I think about how I should have found a way to keep you safe."

"Mom, it isn't your fault," Paige said. She meant it, too. If Adam had done anything for her, it was this: he'd made her confront what she actually felt about her mother. "You're the one who got me out of there. You're the one who believed me, and who gave up everything to keep me safe. You did your best, Mom."

They were both crying now, and Paige held onto her mother's hand until the tears stopped.

"I should come over to visit you soon," Paige said. How long had it been since she'd last visited? Months, at least.

"I'd like that," her mother replied.

Paige was surprised to find that she liked the idea too. She might even have stayed there by her mother's bedside if it weren't for the fact that she could see Christopher approaching down the hall. She'd thought that the FBI agent would go with Adam, and she wouldn't see him again, but here he was.

Paige stood. "Sorry, Mom, it looks like I need to talk to Agent Marriott. I need to step outside, but I won't be long."

She meant it. She'd almost lost her mother and spent the last few years without much contact. It was time to make up for lost time.

For now, though, she went out to meet Christopher in the hall.

"I wasn't expecting to see you here," Paige said.

"Well, someone has to take statements from you and your mother about what happened," Christopher said. "And there are plenty of journalists trying to get in, so someone has to keep them back, and... well, I wanted to tell you that you did a great job, Paige. You'd make an excellent profiler."

"I don't know about that," Paige replied. "People died because I didn't understand what Adam was doing quickly enough."

"And more would have if you weren't the one to work out what was really happening. Take the compliment, Paige."

Paige did her best. It helped that it was coming from Christopher.

"What are your bosses saying about you giving me your gun?" Paige asked.

"For the moment, they aren't asking too many questions. The situation played out well, and the only person hurt is a guy who probably deserves a lot worse."

He did, but Paige hadn't deserved to have to be the one who did it. She hadn't left Adam alive for his sake, but for her own.

"Have you thought about what you'll do next?" Christopher asked.

Paige shrugged. "I think I've had enough excitement for a while. I'm going to go home and finish my thesis. I guess there are going to be some parts of it I'll need to rework."

"Maybe," Christopher said. "On the other hand, I'm pretty sure that catching Riker counts as proof that at least some of what you're thinking about him is on the right lines."

Paige hoped so.

"It was good working with you, Agent Marriott," she said.

"You too, Ms. King. And maybe next time I see you, it will be *Doctor* King."

"You think you'll see me again?" Paige asked.

Christopher smiled then. "I hope so."

*

The rewrites to Paige's thesis weren't going well. It turned out that there was nothing worse for a PhD thesis than a last-minute shift in perspective, because it meant that almost everything had to be reworked. Paige couldn't leave it as it was, though, not after everything that had happened.

There were whole sections to add on the things that had happened since Adam's escape, and on the ways that he'd obviously manipulated her during the sessions.

Paige wasn't managing to write them yet, though, because she found that she couldn't focus. Other thoughts kept distracting her. Some were of her mom, hoping that she was ok. Some were of Christopher, because wife or not, gone from her life or not, it still felt as if they'd forged some kind of connection working on the case that went deep.

Her phone rang. It was Prof. Thornton. Paige answered quickly.

"Hey, is everything ok?" she asked.

"Better than ok, Paige," he said. "I have some great news for you."

Paige frowned, not quite knowing what to expect. "What kind of great news?"

"I was talking to a couple of friends about your work, and they're very impressed. They have a research project running on criminal psychology, and they're looking for a postdoc to work with them conducting inmate interviews. They'd like to talk to you about the job."

A couple of weeks ago, that would have been exactly the kind of news Paige wanted to hear more than anything. It would have been a step along the route to her dreams, and exactly the kind of first step on the ladder in academia that she knew was so hard to find.

Now, though, she found herself hesitating.

"Paige?" Prof. Thornton said. "Did you hear me?"

"I heard," Paige said. "Sorry, I'm still trying to process this."

Before, she wouldn't have needed to process. Now, though, it felt as though everything that had happened in the last few days had woken

165

something up in her. A shift in who she was, or maybe just in what she wanted.

Now, Paige found herself thinking about what Christopher had said about her making a good profiler. Something about that felt right, congruent. Like it was a missing piece of something that Paige had been waiting for.

"That's understandable," Prof. Thornton said. "I'm sure I can hold them off for a day or so if you need some time. But this really is a good opportunity, Paige."

"It is," Paige agreed. Then she said the part that seemed obvious to her now, even if it wouldn't have before. "But I don't want it."

"You don't want it?"

"I want... all of this has shown me that I want to do something else," Paige said. "I want to do some good with my work. I want... I want to become a profiler."

She knew in that moment that, as soon as she finished her thesis, Paige was going to apply to join the FBI. She understood serial killers as well as anyone else out there, but what use was that knowledge if she didn't use it to stop them?

Maybe it would even put her in a position where she could finally look for the serial killer who had touched her life so sharply when she was a girl.

Maybe, just maybe, she would finally be able to find the man who had killed her father.

THE GIRL HE CHOSE
(A Paige King FBI Suspense Thriller—Book 2)

Paige King, after receiving her Ph.D. in forensic psychology, has been asked to join the FBI's elite BAU unit. When a deranged killer on death row seems to know more than he lets on about an active case, Paige is summoned to enter his mind and crack the case—before the final hours that lead to his execution.

"A masterpiece of thriller and mystery."
—Books and Movie Reviews, Roberto Mattos (re *Once Gone*)

THE GIRL HE CHOSE is book #2 in a new series by #1 bestselling and critically acclaimed mystery and suspense author Blake Pierce.

The death row killer's clues soon lead Paige down a rabbit hole of red herrings and dead ends, and time is running out for her to save the next victim.

Can she piece the clues together in time?

Or has she finally met her match?

A complex psychological crime thriller full of twists and turns and packed with heart-pounding suspense, the PAIGE KING mystery series will make you fall in love with a brilliant new female protagonist and keep you turning pages late into the night.

Book #3 in the series—THE GIRL HE TOOK—is now also available.

"An edge of your seat thriller in a new series that keeps you turning pages! ...So many twists, turns and red herrings... I can't wait to see what happens next."

—Reader review (*Her Last Wish*)

"A strong, complex story about two FBI agents trying to stop a serial killer. If you want an author to capture your attention and have you guessing, yet trying to put the pieces together, Pierce is your author!"
—Reader review (*Her Last Wish*)

"A typical Blake Pierce twisting, turning, roller coaster ride suspense thriller. Will have you turning the pages to the last sentence of the last chapter!!!"
—Reader review (*City of Prey*)

"Right from the start we have an unusual protagonist that I haven't seen done in this genre before. The action is nonstop... A very atmospheric novel that will keep you turning pages well into the wee hours."
—Reader review (*City of Prey*)

"Everything that I look for in a book... a great plot, interesting characters, and grabs your interest right away. The book moves along at a breakneck pace and stays that way until the end. Now on go I to book two!"
—Reader review (*Girl, Alone*)

"Exciting, heart pounding, edge of your seat book... a must read for mystery and suspense readers!"
—Reader review (*Girl, Alone*)

Blake Pierce

Blake Pierce is the USA Today bestselling author of the RILEY PAGE mystery series, which includes seventeen books. Blake Pierce is also the author of the MACKENZIE WHITE mystery series, comprising fourteen books; of the AVERY BLACK mystery series, comprising six books; of the KERI LOCKE mystery series, comprising five books; of the MAKING OF RILEY PAIGE mystery series, comprising six books; of the KATE WISE mystery series, comprising seven books; of the CHLOE FINE psychological suspense mystery, comprising six books; of the JESSE HUNT psychological suspense thriller series, comprising twenty four books; of the AU PAIR psychological suspense thriller series, comprising three books; of the ZOE PRIME mystery series, comprising six books; of the ADELE SHARP mystery series, comprising fifteen books, of the EUROPEAN VOYAGE cozy mystery series, comprising four books; of the new LAURA FROST FBI suspense thriller, comprising nine books (and counting); of the new ELLA DARK FBI suspense thriller, comprising eleven books (and counting); of the A YEAR IN EUROPE cozy mystery series, comprising nine books, of the AVA GOLD mystery series, comprising six books (and counting); of the RACHEL GIFT mystery series, comprising six books (and counting); of the VALERIE LAW mystery series, comprising three books (and counting); and of the PAIGE KING mystery series, comprising three books (and counting).

An avid reader and lifelong fan of the mystery and thriller genres, Blake loves to hear from you, so please feel free to visit www.blakepierceauthor.com to learn more and stay in touch.

BOOKS BY BLAKE PIERCE

PAIGE KING MYSTERY SERIES
THE GIRL HE PINED (Book #1)
THE GIRL HE CHOSE (Book #2)
THE GIRL HE TOOK (Book #3)

VALERIE LAW MYSTERY SERIES
NO MERCY (Book #1)
NO PITY (Book #2)
NO FEAR (Book #3

RACHEL GIFT MYSTERY SERIES
HER LAST WISH (Book #1)
HER LAST CHANCE (Book #2)
HER LAST HOPE (Book #3)
HER LAST FEAR (Book #4)
HER LAST CHOICE (Book #5)
HER LAST BREATH (Book #6)

AVA GOLD MYSTERY SERIES
CITY OF PREY (Book #1)
CITY OF FEAR (Book #2)
CITY OF BONES (Book #3)
CITY OF GHOSTS (Book #4)
CITY OF DEATH (Book #5)
CITY OF VICE (Book #6)

A YEAR IN EUROPE
A MURDER IN PARIS (Book #1)
DEATH IN FLORENCE (Book #2)
VENGEANCE IN VIENNA (Book #3)
A FATALITY IN SPAIN (Book #4)

ELLA DARK FBI SUSPENSE THRILLER
GIRL, ALONE (Book #1)

GIRL, TAKEN (Book #2)
GIRL, HUNTED (Book #3)
GIRL, SILENCED (Book #4)
GIRL, VANISHED (Book 5)
GIRL ERASED (Book #6)
GIRL, FORSAKEN (Book #7)
GIRL, TRAPPED (Book #8)
GIRL, EXPENDABLE (Book #9)
GIRL, ESCAPED (Book #10)
GIRL, HIS (Book #11)

LAURA FROST FBI SUSPENSE THRILLER
ALREADY GONE (Book #1)
ALREADY SEEN (Book #2)
ALREADY TRAPPED (Book #3)
ALREADY MISSING (Book #4)
ALREADY DEAD (Book #5)
ALREADY TAKEN (Book #6)
ALREADY CHOSEN (Book #7)
ALREADY LOST (Book #8)
ALREADY HIS (Book #9)

EUROPEAN VOYAGE COZY MYSTERY SERIES
MURDER (AND BAKLAVA) (Book #1)
DEATH (AND APPLE STRUDEL) (Book #2)
CRIME (AND LAGER) (Book #3)
MISFORTUNE (AND GOUDA) (Book #4)
CALAMITY (AND A DANISH) (Book #5)
MAYHEM (AND HERRING) (Book #6)

ADELE SHARP MYSTERY SERIES
LEFT TO DIE (Book #1)
LEFT TO RUN (Book #2)
LEFT TO HIDE (Book #3)
LEFT TO KILL (Book #4)
LEFT TO MURDER (Book #5)
LEFT TO ENVY (Book #6)
LEFT TO LAPSE (Book #7)
LEFT TO VANISH (Book #8)

LEFT TO HUNT (Book #9)
LEFT TO FEAR (Book #10)
LEFT TO PREY (Book #11)
LEFT TO LURE (Book #12)
LEFT TO CRAVE (Book #13)
LEFT TO LOATHE (Book #14)
LEFT TO HARM (Book #15)

THE AU PAIR SERIES
ALMOST GONE (Book#1)
ALMOST LOST (Book #2)
ALMOST DEAD (Book #3)

ZOE PRIME MYSTERY SERIES
FACE OF DEATH (Book#1)
FACE OF MURDER (Book #2)
FACE OF FEAR (Book #3)
FACE OF MADNESS (Book #4)
FACE OF FURY (Book #5)
FACE OF DARKNESS (Book #6)

A JESSIE HUNT PSYCHOLOGICAL SUSPENSE SERIES
THE PERFECT WIFE (Book #1)
THE PERFECT BLOCK (Book #2)
THE PERFECT HOUSE (Book #3)
THE PERFECT SMILE (Book #4)
THE PERFECT LIE (Book #5)
THE PERFECT LOOK (Book #6)
THE PERFECT AFFAIR (Book #7)
THE PERFECT ALIBI (Book #8)
THE PERFECT NEIGHBOR (Book #9)
THE PERFECT DISGUISE (Book #10)
THE PERFECT SECRET (Book #11)
THE PERFECT FAÇADE (Book #12)
THE PERFECT IMPRESSION (Book #13)
THE PERFECT DECEIT (Book #14)
THE PERFECT MISTRESS (Book #15)
THE PERFECT IMAGE (Book #16)
THE PERFECT VEIL (Book #17)

THE PERFECT INDISCRETION (Book #18)
THE PERFECT RUMOR (Book #19)
THE PERFECT COUPLE (Book #20)
THE PERFECT MURDER (Book #21)
THE PERFECT HUSBAND (Book #22)
THE PERFECT SCANDAL (Book #23)
THE PERFECT MASK (Book #24)

CHLOE FINE PSYCHOLOGICAL SUSPENSE SERIES
NEXT DOOR (Book #1)
A NEIGHBOR'S LIE (Book #2)
CUL DE SAC (Book #3)
SILENT NEIGHBOR (Book #4)
HOMECOMING (Book #5)
TINTED WINDOWS (Book #6)

KATE WISE MYSTERY SERIES
IF SHE KNEW (Book #1)
IF SHE SAW (Book #2)
IF SHE RAN (Book #3)
IF SHE HID (Book #4)
IF SHE FLED (Book #5)
IF SHE FEARED (Book #6)
IF SHE HEARD (Book #7)

THE MAKING OF RILEY PAIGE SERIES
WATCHING (Book #1)
WAITING (Book #2)
LURING (Book #3)
TAKING (Book #4)
STALKING (Book #5)
KILLING (Book #6)

RILEY PAIGE MYSTERY SERIES
ONCE GONE (Book #1)
ONCE TAKEN (Book #2)
ONCE CRAVED (Book #3)
ONCE LURED (Book #4)

ONCE HUNTED (Book #5)
ONCE PINED (Book #6)
ONCE FORSAKEN (Book #7)
ONCE COLD (Book #8)
ONCE STALKED (Book #9)
ONCE LOST (Book #10)
ONCE BURIED (Book #11)
ONCE BOUND (Book #12)
ONCE TRAPPED (Book #13)
ONCE DORMANT (Book #14)
ONCE SHUNNED (Book #15)
ONCE MISSED (Book #16)
ONCE CHOSEN (Book #17)

MACKENZIE WHITE MYSTERY SERIES
BEFORE HE KILLS (Book #1)
BEFORE HE SEES (Book #2)
BEFORE HE COVETS (Book #3)
BEFORE HE TAKES (Book #4)
BEFORE HE NEEDS (Book #5)
BEFORE HE FEELS (Book #6)
BEFORE HE SINS (Book #7)
BEFORE HE HUNTS (Book #8)
BEFORE HE PREYS (Book #9)
BEFORE HE LONGS (Book #10)
BEFORE HE LAPSES (Book #11)
BEFORE HE ENVIES (Book #12)
BEFORE HE STALKS (Book #13)
BEFORE HE HARMS (Book #14)

AVERY BLACK MYSTERY SERIES
CAUSE TO KILL (Book #1)
CAUSE TO RUN (Book #2)
CAUSE TO HIDE (Book #3)
CAUSE TO FEAR (Book #4)
CAUSE TO SAVE (Book #5)
CAUSE TO DREAD (Book #6)

KERI LOCKE MYSTERY SERIES

Made in the USA
Las Vegas, NV
09 September 2022

54953291R00105